9·14·06

LG

HIDE AND SEEK

Keeping low, Slocum scuttled to the fence, under it, then to the base of the hill and along that base. When he heard a scuffing sound, he stopped dead and listened hard.

There it was again. Someone was making their way toward his old position, about thirty feet up the hill from where he presently stood.

He moved over a couple of feet, taking cover behind a scraggly sage, then held very still, alert for the slightest sound.

Suddenly, Carlito stood up from nowhere—Slocum thought he must be part Apache!—and wheeled to fire behind him . . .

JAKE LOGAN

SLOCUM AND THE BORDER WAR

JOVE BOOKS, NEW YORK

THE BERKLEY PUBLISHING GROUP
Published by the Penguin Group
Penguin Group (USA) Inc.
375 Hudson Street, New York, New York 10014, USA
Penguin Group (Canada), 90 Eglinton Avenue East, Suite 700, Toronto, Ontario M4P 2Y3, Canada
(a division of Pearson Penguin Canada Inc.)
Penguin Books Ltd., 80 Strand, London WC2R 0RL, England
Penguin Group Ireland, 25 St. Stephen's Green, Dublin 2, Ireland (a division of Penguin Books Ltd.)
Penguin Group (Australia), 250 Camberwell Road, Camberwell, Victoria 3124, Australia
(a division of Pearson Australia Group Pty. Ltd.)
Penguin Books India Pvt. Ltd., 11 Community Centre, Panchsheel Park, New Delhi—110 017, India
Penguin Group (NZ), Cnr. Airborne and Rosedale Roads, Albany, Auckland 1310, New Zealand
(a division of Pearson New Zealand Ltd.)
Penguin Books (South Africa) (Pty.) Ltd., 24 Sturdee Avenue, Rosebank, Johannesburg 2196, South Africa

Penguin Books Ltd., Registered Offices: 80 Strand, London WC2R 0RL, England

SLOCUM AND THE BORDER WAR

A Jove Book / published by arrangement with the author

PRINTING HISTORY
Jove edition / August 2006

For information, address: The Berkley Publishing Group,
a division of Penguin Group (USA) Inc.,
375 Hudson Street, New York, New York 10014.

ISBN: 0-515-14047-3

JOVE®
Jove Books are published by The Berkley Publishing Group,
a division of Penguin Group (USA) Inc.,
375 Hudson Street, New York, New York 10014.
JOVE is a registered trademark of Penguin Group (USA) Inc.
The "J" design is a trademark belonging to Penguin Group (USA) Inc.

PRINTED IN THE UNITED STATES OF AMERICA

10 9 8 7 6 5 4 3 2 1

1

Slocum headed down through the Arizona Territory to the border country. He'd been asked by Ralph MacCorkendale, a fellow he'd met about three years back, to come down and quell a little "disagreement" about the ownership of some cattle that carried MacCorkendale's brand.

MacCorkendale thought he owned them. Pablo Valdez, another rancher just across the border, seemed to think that anything that wandered into Mexico was his, regardless of the brand it carried.

MacCorkendale was more than a tad vexed about it.

And rightly so.

They had tried negotiations, they had tried hiring muscle, and now things had gotten serious. MacCorkendale had hired Slocum.

Valdez had called in Jorgé Rodriguez.

Now, Slocum had dealt with Rodriguez before. First, he'd fought alongside him during the Pleasant Valley War, next he'd fought against him in Silver Springs, and the last time they met up, he'd played cards with him. All nice and amiable.

Rodriguez was a good partner in a fight and a worse opponent. Slocum was hoping that Señor Valdez could be convinced of the error of his ways before somebody got killed.

Especially if that somebody was him.

All that aside, there was someone down in the borderlands that Slocum felt a need to see: one Señorita Maria Anna Lopez.

She owned and ran Cantina Lopez all by herself these days, her papa having died five years back. She was sloe-eyed, copper-skinned, had straight hair as black as a raven's wing and so long it covered her butt, and a figure that wouldn't quit.

He could span her waist with both his hands, he remembered.

He hadn't seen her for over a year and was eager for some time spent in her company.

As he rode along on Concho, his tall, black-spotted, leopard Appaloosa gelding, he amused himself by wondering if she still lived upstairs, over the cantina, and if she still had that round table up there, the one by the windows, where they'd made love the last time.

Did she still have poreless, flawless skin and those legs—oh, those legs!—that went on forever? A man could spend an eternity wrapped in those legs.

Were her breasts as round as he remembered, as plump and full and tipped in those sienna nipples that hardened and peaked at his slightest touch? Was her backside still as round and muscular, yet soft and pliable?

Was she married?

That last question, which had crept in from who knows where, sent a shudder through him—enough so that the horse beneath him felt it and gave a little nervous hop.

He put a hand on the Appy's neck. "It's all right, Concho, just me bein' silly."

The horse snorted and resumed his pace, and Slocum gave a shake to his head. Married! No, she wouldn't have gotten married, not Maria. She had a business to run! She was independent, strong!

But then, running that cantina would be a lot easier with a husband to do half the work, wouldn't it?

Or maybe she'd actually fallen in love.

Part of Slocum—the vain part—doubted that she could ever love another man. After being with him, that was. But the other part knew it was a real possibility.

Maria was a beautiful girl who owned property, a business. He had a feeling she'd spent the last year being the target of every horny caballero and cowboy in the district.

Part of the joy went out of him. His face set into a scowl.

Well, if it's to be, then it's to be, he thought and urged Concho into a lope. MacCorkendale was waiting.

Maria Anna Lopez, the sloe-eyed beauty who lived upstairs over her cantina, smiled warmly at the vaquero who had just touched her—quite by accident, although with questionable intent—in what she considered a highly inappropriate manner, and then brought down the wooden chair she held over her head.

Very hard.

She was very strong for a girl.

The chair was no longer recognizable as furniture, but the vaquero—although unconscious—was still a vaquero.

Some of the other customers shrank back. Still others, who knew her, ignored the entire proceeding.

She brushed her hands on her full, white skirts, although they weren't really dirty, and said, "Diego! Take out this trash!"

From the back, out of the kitchen, came Diego, a short man—a little pudgy, she had always thought, but very strong—with a mustache and a balding head, who leaned over, picked up the vaquero's booted feet, and dragged him toward the front door.

He didn't say a word.

He didn't ask a question.

She liked that in an employee.

Come to think of it, she liked that in a man.

Well, most of them.

About the time Diego came back in, she turned and walked behind the bar. She or Diego usually tended the bar themselves. Otherwise, too many "complimentary" whiskeys seemed to get handed out, and the cerveza tended to run a little too freely.

She didn't allow trouble in her cantina, she kept a close eye on the cash box, and she had never, ever let a man become more important that Cantina Lopez.

Well, except one.

She had no time for a family of her own. She had a niece and nephew to take care of, a mother that needed to be fed and clothed, a drunk of a sister that needed watching, and a brother-in-law best not spoken of.

She was one very good businesswoman, was Maria Anna Lopez. She had to be.

Slocum rode into the MacCorkendale place, the Bar M Ranch: a curious affair, for although the outbuildings were constructed from adobe bricks, the house itself was built entirely of wood. Odd, in adobe territory. Slocum wondered where he'd found the wood to put the place up!

There were few men around, which surprised him, but he decided they must be out on the range. Those who remained eyed him curiously but gave him a wide berth. No one said a word to him as he rode through the yard and up to the house.

Now, the house was huge, and Victorian in style—all gingerbread trim and brightly, wildly painted in blues and greens and tans and orange and white—and probably three stories, if you counted the turret. Which, of course, he did.

He tied Concho to the porch rail, climbed the steps to the wraparound porch, and knocked on the front door, which was heavy with ornate, leaded glass.

A moment passed before a blond girl answered, curtsied, and said, "You must be Mr. Slocum?" in a thick German accent. Slocum nodded in the affirmative, his eyes taking a quick inventory.

She was a little on the stout side, pretty enough, with freckles and blue eyes. Yellow pigtails were wound elaborately into a kind of bun contraption on her head. A long, white apron succeeded in covering what figure she might have had, and she carried a very serious expression. *Sturdy* was his snap judgment.

"Yes'm, that I am," he replied when he found that she was just going to stand there, blocking the door. "MacCorkendale around?"

She stared up at him, not blinking, not giving a single sign of what she thought of him, if anything, and then she said, "*Ja.* You wait in parlor." And moved aside.

He took it as an invitation and stepped in.

The house was surprisingly dark and cool, filled with deep mahogany furniture and goldfish bowls and potted ferns and what Slocum thought were some very good oil paintings of ships at sea or racehorses or the occasional still life. All in all, the place fairly reeked of New York, or maybe Europe, and seemed completely out of place here on the Arizona desert.

The girl led him to the right, into the parlor, pointed him toward a dark brown leather chair, and said, "I get Mr. MacCorkendale." She curtsied and was gone.

Belatedly, Slocum removed his hat and tossed it to a tabletop. He sat and stared at a painting of a full-masted schooner plowing the seas until the doors slid open again, and MacCorkendale walked in.

In contrast to his house, MacCorkendale was all Westerner. He was dressed in Levi's, a worn, blue work shirt, dusty boots that tracked faint white streaks over the dark, highly polished wooden floors, and was presently mopping his brow and the back of his neck with a soggy-looking red bandanna.

He was leaner than Slocum remembered him, but he still had a full head of salt-and-pepper hair, an open face with a ready grin, and sparkling blue eyes. He'd left his hat someplace, but the suntan line across the center of his forehead marked the angle at which he usually wore it.

He grinned right off and said, "Slocum!" in that big, booming voice and stuck out a paw. As they shook hands, he said, "Glad to see you! Mighty fine, mighty fine! Get you a drink and a cigar?"

"Pleased," replied Slocum, who was lucky to get the word in.

"Suppose you're wonderin' about the house," MacCorkendale went on as he moved toward a small bar in the corner. "Ain't to my taste, I gotta tell you, but the wife, well . . . you know. No, I don't reckon you do . . ."

He poured three fingers of scotch whiskey into a crystal glass, pulled a cigar from the humidor, and handed both to Slocum before pouring himself a drink.

Slocum bit off the end of the cigar—which turned out to be a very fine Havana—before he asked, somewhat incredulously, "You get married, MacCorkendale?"

"Hell, yes," MacCorkendale said, taking a seat opposite Slocum. "Two years ago last November. Hell of a gal. You met her. Helga."

The woman at the door? Slocum had taken her for a maid! He said, "The blond gal?"

"That's her!"

With his thumbnail, Slocum popped a lucifer into flame and lit his cigar, puffing on it longer than was necessary before he said, "Nice catch, MacCorkendale. Pretty gal." He could imagine as much fire coming from her in the bedroom as a pan of cold water.

MacCorkendale was enthusiastic, though, and went on. "Oh, yeah, she's pretty and smart, real smart. Knows about all kinds of things!" He checked the hall to make sure she wasn't listening.

"I let her pick the plan for this place from a catalogue," he went on, "and I'll be damned if they didn't ship it out here! I mean, they sent the whole blasted house—in pieces!"

He stopped to bark out a laugh. "Why, my boys had to put it together like a jigsaw puzzle—course, there were instructions—and I thought it was damn silly, and I'd been a pure-D fool. I mean, don't it seem a little like a duck in a henhouse to you? Just did it to humor her, you know? But now, by God, I think it's grand!"

The pride in MacCorkendale's voice was overwhelming, and Slocum nodded in agreement, even though he would have likened it more to a hog in a henhouse. Maybe it would grow on him. But he doubted it.

He took a sip of his scotch. "So, tell me more about this trouble you're having with Pablo Valdez, MacCorkendale."

2

Ralph MacCorkendale was forthright, if nothing else. Slocum heard his story, had made his excuses for dinner, and was on his way to town, all within the space of forty minutes.

MacCorkendale hadn't told him anything he hadn't already known—or suspected—about Valdez or his hired gun, Rodriguez. And the smells coming from the kitchen were . . . less than appetizing, although MacCorkendale swore up and down that his Helga was the finest cook in the whole damned county.

But Slocum already knew the best damn cook in the county—in fact, the gal who was just about the best at everything important—and wanted to hie himself to her cantina pronto.

So he did.

He rode into Jaguar Hole at a soft jog, tied Concho beside the water trough at the rail in front of Cantina Lopez, said a silent prayer that she was still there and still single—and willing—and pushed through the swinging batwing doors.

There wasn't much of a crowd inside—but then, he hadn't exactly expected a mob at three in the afternoon on a Wednesday. He didn't see Maria right away. There was a balding Mexican man at the bar and a few patrons scattered at the tables in the shadows.

He went to the bar and ordered a cerveza. While the bartender poured it, he asked, "Maria around?"

The barkeep slid his glass to him from five feet away, lazily rubbed his hands, then the newly sudsy bartop, and said, "Be back very soon. You a friend?"

Slocum nodded. "An old one. Can I get a plate of enchiladas? Beef?"

"Right away, señor," said the man, still without expression, and slid through a door behind the bar and into the back room.

Slocum carried his cerveza to a table and sat with his back to the wall and his boots propped up on another chair. He tipped his hat back and took a long, refreshing drink. Jaguar Hole wasn't a long ride from MacCorkendale's place, but it was sure a dry one. From his vantage point, he could see out the front door, and see Concho still lipping at the trough's water.

The barman brought his food in no time, saying, "I am Diego, señor. If there is anything else you need, I am at your beck and call."

"Gracias, Diego," Slocum said. He slid his boots to the floor and picked up a fork, and in two shakes he was halfway through the first enchilada. They were like he remembered them, packed with shaved beef and onions and peppers, and thickly topped with tangy sauce and cheeses and guacamole.

They were damned good.

He was nearly finished with the second one when a shadow suddenly loomed over his table. He looked up and straight into the face of Jorgé Rodriguez.

Now, if anybody had ever looked like a hired gun, it was old Jorgé. He had a face like an ax blade, bisected by a thick salt-and-pepper mustache. Thick brows beetled over narrowed, jet-black eyes that held a none-too-kindly expression. As usual, he did not smile.

As for his dress, he still favored the white, blousy Mexican pants and shirt and the wide sombrero, along with the worn bandoleros strapped across his chest. In fact, Slocum would have sworn that Rodriguez was still wearing the same clothes he'd worn the last time they'd met.

Slocum swallowed, then said, "See you're still favorin' those old Smith & Wessons, Jorgé. Still carry that Arkansas toothpick down your boot?"

Jorgé's impassive face suddenly bloomed into a grin. "Slocum!" he said in his thickly accented voice, and jerked out a chair of his own. "You are still very funny, for a gringo!" He glanced at Slocum's glass, which was nearly empty, and turned toward the bar. "Diego!" he shouted, and held up two fingers. *"Dos cervezas!"*

Diego nodded and pulled two fresh glasses off the shelf.

"So, amigo," Jorgé continued, "we both know why you have come here."

Slocum nodded and said, "Yeah. The enchiladas are worth the ride, even from Colorado."

This time Jorgé's grin broke into a barking laugh. "Very good joke, Slocum! Yes, the food is *muy bueno*, but you know what I mean. What are we going to do with these two? My employer and yours?"

"Well, seems to me your Señor Valdez could stop swipin' Mr. MacCorkendale's cattle. That'd pretty much put a stop to it."

This time, Jorgé didn't laugh. "You know, compadre, I have tried this approach myself. I say, 'Send Señor MacCorkendale's cattle back, Señor Valdez! You are a rich man with a big rancho and plenty cattle already.' But he says it is a principle. If the cattle are on Mexican soil, they must be Mexican, no matter whose brand they carry."

Jorgé shrugged, as if saying that he'd done his best, and any further effort was impossible.

"So they expect us to settle this thing for 'em," Slocum said, cutting off a bite of his enchilada with the side of his fork. "So, say that one of us kills the other. That gonna settle anything, or will Valdez just hire himself another gun?"

Jorgé grinned wider than before. "You say Valdez will have to hire again? What makes you so sure it will not be MacCorkendale doing the hiring?"

Slocum shrugged. "Just a hunch, Jorgé. Feelin' lucky, I reckon."

Diego brought them their cervezas, which broke the rhythm of the conversation and therefore kept it from escalating into something uglier. Which it very easily could have.

As it was, Jorgé just arched his bushy, caterpillar brows and asked, "Was not it you who told me that men make their own luck, Slocum?"

"I don't recall, Jorgé," Slocum replied, draining his first glass of Mexican beer, "but I hope to hell that it's true."

"Who was dat man, that Slocum?" Helga asked Ralph MacCorkendale as she ladled out his potato soup. Or potato salad. He had never been able to tell the difference, except that one had more vinegar than the other.

"Just that. Slocum," he said, hoping that would end it.

But no such luck. "Who is he?" she asked. She took her seat and passed him a platter of sausages the size of a six-year-old's forearm. "You mention his name many times, Herr MacCorkendale, but you never say why."

"How many times do I got to tell you, honey, you don't call your husband Herr MacCorkendale. My name is Ralph. Use it, okay?"

Although those prim manners were primarily what he'd married her for, he was getting a little fed up with her old-country ways. Not to mention her goddamn potato soup or potato salad or whatever it was, and her sausages and the goddamn Wiener schnitzel.

Why couldn't they have a steak or a plain ham sandwich every once in a while?

"*Ja* . . . Ralph," she said softly, as if the utterance of his Christian name was almost too intimate for her to bear. "Have you hired *Herr* Slocum, or is he just visiting with us?"

He remained silent, and finally, after five or six long minutes, she said, "Herr MacCorkendale, it is not right that you keep things from—"

"Shut up!" he roared, much louder than he'd intended. Much more viciously, too, and she cowered as if he'd hit her, damn it. From the other end of an eight-foot table!

Quickly, he got himself under control and said, "Helga, forgive me. I didn't mean to snap at you, honey. It's just . . . business, that's all. Slocum's here on business. That's all you need to know."

Helga pursed her lips—an annoying little expression, he thought—and after a moment, said, "You are meaning Valdez business, *nicht wahr*?"

"None'a your nevermind," he said, and cut off a bite of her goddamn bratwurst or liverwurst or whatever the hell it was. Donkey dong, that's what he called it. At least to himself. "Now leave it be."

"*Ja, mein Herr,*" she muttered, and spoke no more.

Slocum woke while the last of the afternoon light was still flooding through the windows, casting long shadows on the clean, white linens and highlighting the long, lean, yet ripe cinnamon body drowsing beside him.

He slid his hand along her shoulder, down her torso, and over the bell of her hip, then stopped and dipped his head to kiss the nape of her neck.

"Maria?" he whispered.

She stirred slightly, and he smiled when she rolled toward him, brushing long strands of ebony hair from her face. "You, too, are awake, my Slocum?" she asked lazily, an infectious grin on her face.

"Yes'm," he said and slid his hand across the silky flatness of her belly to her opposite hip. He hoped she was in the mood, because he wanted her again. And not just to take his mind off Jorgé Rodriguez, either.

Damn!

He'd let that ugly sidewinder into his thoughts again! And he'd promised himself that while he was with Maria he wouldn't think of him, think about this stupid range war that was brewing, or allow the personas of Pablo Valdez or Ralph MacCorkendale to enter his mind.

And he'd lost his erection to boot!

This detail hadn't slipped past Maria, either. She said, "Are your thoughts so black, my darling?"

Without waiting for an answer, she slipped her slender hand down his belly, took hold of his withered cock, and began to rhythmically, gently tease him with the pressure and movement of her fingers.

He was hard again in no time.

God, she was a wonder!

She had brought him so far that he was thudding for release, and he pushed her hand away. "That's plenty, honey," he said, his voice throaty with urgency and want.

She batted her eyelashes innocently. "You no like, Señor Slocum?"

"I like, you little spitfire," he said as he moved between her legs and positioned himself. "I like it just fine, and you know it."

She giggled softly and brought up her knees to grip his sides. "Maybe I do," she said, her voice filled with potential chuckles. "Maybe I do not. Maybe you should show me, Slocum, no?"

"Yes, Maria," he said, and entered her. As she sighed and wriggled with pleasure, he said, "Maybe I will."

3

In the dying afternoon light, Jorgé Rodriguez rode slowly back to the rancho of Señor Valdez, pondering his options.

Slocum would be no pushover. He'd known this from the beginning, when Valdez had hired his guns. But after speaking with Slocum, he was certain of it. There could be no negotiations, no compromises.

He feared it would end just as Slocum had said: with one or both of them dead, and more guns paid for and brought in by both sides. It would be endless. It would start a border war.

Jorgé Rodriguez was a pragmatic man, perhaps as much as his old compadre Slocum was. It seemed the only fools in the mix were the men they were working for. Particularly Pablo Valdez. It was Valdez's stubbornness that was the cause of all of this.

Jorgé did not blame Señor MacCorkendale for wanting his own cattle back. Valdez was stealing them and using the border as his excuse.

What to do, what to do . . .

Jorgé had hired his gun to many men in his time, and he had always fought until the end. That was the point of it, wasn't it? Right or wrong, he had always stayed, once he'd given his word.

His word was very important to Jorgé Rodriguez.

His horse, Zorro, shied violently to the left, but Jorgé sat him. "It's only a covey of quail, amigo," he said as the last few stragglers flew up. "What is wrong with you this fine afternoon, to be so touchy?"

He soothed the gelding with long strokes down the horse's glossy, black neck, then sent him on his way again. Odd for Zorro to be jumpy like that. He was usually a very calm, well-trained horse.

But perhaps he had picked up on Jorgé's unease after the conversation with Slocum. Jorgé had plenty enough to share, anyway. In fact, the more he thought about it, the more distressed he became.

He liked Slocum. Admired him. And he'd certainly hate to kill him.

On the other hand, he didn't particularly wish to be dead, himself.

"Aye, yi, yi," he said softly, patting the black gelding's neck. "It is—how do you say, Zorro? A conundrum. I must think of something clever. Or Slocum must."

Somehow, he didn't think it would be him.

Finally, Maria had to go downstairs and mind the cantina, but Slocum hung around. He had an all-night invitation, after all, and what kind of idiot would throw that away?

There wasn't much to see in Jaguar Hole, however, and once he took a walking tour of all three blocks of the town, just to stretch his legs a bit, and then put up Concho in the livery, about the only thing left was to go back to Cantina Lopez and order a cerveza and some supper to soak it up.

The crowd was much more sizable than it had been earlier in the day. Folks must make a special trip to come to Jaguar Hole just to eat Maria's chow, he decided. He figured there were more folks in the cantina than the entire population of Jaguar Hole, and the hotel had been the only building of any size that he'd seen during his tour.

He also thought it odd that a town this small had livery stalls for fourteen horses and turnouts for two dozen more.

And they'd been mostly full. He'd gotten Concho the next to the last stall.

The crowd in the cantina wasn't all that rowdy—at least, not nearly so rowdy as he would have expected. And he figured that Maria had a good bit to do with this. He watched her behind the bar, drawing cerveza and pouring whiskey, passing out pickles, eggs, and peanuts, and calling orders back to the kitchen.

Everything ran like clockwork, and no ungentlemanly behavior was accepted. At all. All the patrons, to a man, called her Señorita Maria or Miss Maria. But they all had that faraway, dreamy look in their eyes when she turned away from them.

She was a powerfully beautiful woman. And an imposing one, as well. Slocum castigated himself for worrying that she might be married. Everybody in the place—except him, it seemed—was terrified of her. Or rather, they were in such awe of her that they'd never, ever, take a chance on romancing her.

Slocum couldn't figure that nobody had ever tried, but mayhap they'd found themselves carried or booted or dragged out into the street faster than they could say, "I love you."

Those treated in such a fashion would usually remember not to repeat the offense.

At eight o'clock—or thereabouts—a mariachi band started to play. Now, if there was one kind of music that Slocum really didn't like, it was mariachi. They always seemed to be off-key and proud if it, playing as loudly as humanly possible. These fellows sang, too—mostly on key, which came as a pleasant surprise—and were a great hit with most of the patrons.

Slocum changed his cervaza orders to whiskeys, and lived through the music. Slowly, the crowd drifted out, thinned, and at two in the morning, Maria sent the last of the customers home.

Excepting Slocum, of course.

By this time, he was pretty damned drunk, having downed five cervezas and at least ten shots of whiskey—actually, he'd lost count—since sundown. He remembered something about Maria coaxing him up and out of his chair, and then having some difficulty navigating the narrow stairs.

He made it all the way to her bedroom, however, before he passed out.

When he woke the next morning, the clock said ten thirty, and the bed was rumpled, but Maria was nowhere in sight.

Dammit, anyhow! Well that would teach him to hang around all night, just waiting and drinking. Today he'd have to get down to work, and if he could get back to town, he was going to limit himself to one—no, make that two—cervezas.

He sat up, his head pounding, and clamped his hands across his forehead. Nobody could complain about Maria watering the whiskey, that was for certain!

He finally made it downstairs at about eleven thirty, at which time Maria—who must have heard him thumping around upstairs—had breakfast ready and waiting for him, along with a pot of good black coffee. She was a good woman.

He downed three cups of coffee before he dug into his sausage and eggs, and consumed all of it while he watched Maria, in the kitchen, cooking. Or rather, he watched the occasional swish of her turquoise skirts as she traveled back and forth from the table to the oven and back again, and the play of her slim, brown calves and mocassin-covered feet.

And he kicked himself about every three minutes for getting so drunk and passing out the night before.

He was just eating the last of his cinnamon sticks when she came out and sat down opposite him, with her arms folded on the table and a grin on her face. "And how do you feel this morning, my handsome American cowboy?"

"Better than I have a right to," he admitted sheepishly.

She leaned forward across the table, and her low neckline exposed the shadows he should have explored the night before.

"Yes, my darling," she said. "You were in very bad shape. I put something in your coffee to make you feel better. Do you?"

He realized he did, and grinned at her. "You little sneak. Yeah, I do. What you put in it, anyhow?"

She shook her finger at him. "Secret family recipe. Like my enchiladas, only different." And then she smiled. "I might tell you one day, Slocum, if you are very, very nice to me."

He maintained his grin, although perhaps it grew a little more salacious. "Oh, I will be, baby. I will be."

Actually, he felt not only better, but a little bit *better* than better, if that were possible. Oh, well. He drank the last of his coffee, set the mug down, and said, "It's back to business for me. I'll see you tonight, honey, if I can get back to town by dark."

"You had better, my Slocum," she said, and winked before she stood up.

He did, too. And when he finished watching her beautiful backside on its way to the kitchen, he kicked himself all the way to the livery stable.

Concho was in fine fettle and ready to get going, and after Slocum brushed his coat into a glossy sheen of black starry spots on the silver-white background, he tacked him up, swung up into the saddle, and set off.

But not toward the MacCorkendale place. He'd decided to visit Pablo Valdez first. Jorgé Rodriguez hadn't been able to talk any sense into him, but where Jorgé had failed, perhaps he could succeed.

It was a long ride down to the Valdez rancho, and Slocum was feeling increasingly . . . odd. He'd never felt quite like this in the aftermath of a hangover before, and the only thing he could lay the blame on was Maria's whatever-it-was. The stuff in the coffee. A man being too drunk to make love wasn't worth a poisoning, was it? Or was it?

He shook his head, and the desert wobbled most disconcertingly. He kept Concho moving, but he closed his eyes for a moment and waited for things to settle back to normalcy. When he cracked one eye open, things seemed to be back to usual, and he opened the other.

It was a calm, windless day, clear-skied and warm and sunny, and he was traveling through a long, wide valley. He'd been riding through it, in fact, for about two hours now, and the end was still nowhere in sight. Yet the breeze made by his passing seemed like cyclone winds, and the sounds of insects and birds and the rustles of snakes and lizards seemed all too close.

He was feeling sick to his stomach and realized that he was a whole lot jumpier than usual, too.

What had she fed him? Poison? Ground glass? Ladanum?

No, no, not Maria. Not his baby, his little Mexican spitfire.

Spitfire. That got him thinking, too.

He felt a stab of pain go through his shoulder before he heard the shot. He heard it echo off the canyon walls, too, as he fell off Concho's side and into the sparse yellow weeds.

Concho stopped immediately and nosed him.

Instinctively drawing his gun, Slocum tried to figure where the shot had come from, but in his fuddled condition he'd lost track of which way he'd been headed.

At last he managed to ascertain that from the direction of the sun, and got off two shots at the cliffs ahead and to the right.

There was no return fire. He must have been down longer than he thought and had been given up for dead. But Jorgé wouldn't bushwhack him, and Jorgé wouldn't just ride off without checking his body, either.

What the hell was going on?

He climbed up to one hand and his knees, favoring his wounded shoulder, and promptly emptied his stomach into the weeds. There wasn't much left, just some canteen water and what remained of the very tail end of his breakfast. And after he vomited, he didn't feel much better.

He forced himself to his feet, then felt his shoulder.

It wasn't bad. He could still move it and didn't hear anything grating around in there, so he figured he hadn't broken any bones. But still, he'd need to get that slug pried out.

And somehow, he didn't think that Valdez's place was the spot to have it done.

As badly as he wanted to get back to Maria's, he was afraid she'd give him some more of her "secret painkiller," and he needed that like he needed another slug in his shoulder.

He'd go back to MacCorkendale's place and see how Helga MacCorkendale was at patching up wounds.

Slowly, while the desert danced around him, he mounted Concho and eased himself into the creaking saddle, and turned the gelding back to the north, out of the canyon and toward Ralph MacCorkendale's ranch.

4

"Helga!" Ralph MacCorkendale shouted when he saw a slumped-over Slocum riding slowly into the yard.

"Wie gehts?" she called back from the kitchen. Probably she was making more hot potato salad and donkey dong, he thought, disgusted.

But he said, "It's Slocum. I think he's hurt. Least, he's got a lot of blood on him!" MacCorkendale yanked open the door and rushed outside, all the while cursing Valdez and his men.

He eased Slocum down from the saddle, and Slocum just stood there, glassy-eyed and shifting his weight from foot to foot. MacCorkendale grabbed the Appy's reins with one hand and propped up Slocum with the other, and started toward the porch.

Helga was just coming out the door. She didn't need any instruction. She ran straight out to them, insinuated herself between her husband and Slocum until she was carrying nearly his entire weight, save what Slocum took himself on his own two feet.

Without looking up at him, she said, "Herr MacCorkendale, put horse away. I see to this."

MacCorkendale stood and watched as she carefully

guided Slocum to the porch steps, then urged him up them and into the house.

Sometimes he couldn't figure women at all.

Not for goddamn beans.

Slocum awoke to the sound of a woman's hum, and also to quite a bit more pain than he'd been feeling previously. It was night. He was in a dark bedroom that wasn't Maria's, and it took him a moment to remember just where he was and what had happened.

"Mrs. MacCorkendale?" he croaked in a voice that didn't sound a bit like his own. He dimly recalled riding into the MacCorkendale ranch.

The humming stopped, and a cool hand touched his forehead. "*Ja,* Herr Slocum. You are safe, now. I dug the bullet from your shoulder."

Mustering the only German he knew, he said, "*Dank.*"

"You were with the luck, Herr Slocum," she went on. "The bullet, it impacted nothing important. I am sure you are very sore, though."

Nodding hurt him, so he said, "Yes," and then, "Water?"

She produced a pitcher and poured him a glass. He drank it down, then asked for more, with which he was supplied.

"Herr Valdez, his men have done this." It wasn't a question.

Slocum, who still thought there might be a way to salvage this situation without starting a border war, set his glass down and said, "No ma'am. Could'a been bandits. Could'a been anybody. They—I mean he—was too far off for me to see."

She nodded. "You are a very cautious man, I think."

He mustered a smile. "Yes ma'am."

"I go get Herr MacCorkendale now. He wished to speak with you when you awakened. And I will bring you some supper."

She went out the door, letting in a glow of lantern light, and left it open behind her. Slocum listened to the soft tread of her shoes down the hallway runner, and after a moment, MacCorkendale's sharp, clipped bootsteps drawing near.

He burst in the door, shouting, "Damn it, Slocum! That Mex dog is lower than a well digger's boot, sendin' his men out to bushwhack you! Helga says you'll be fine, but goddamn! You see what I'm up against, now? Won't listen to reason, won't listen to anybody! He's a thief and now practically a murderer, and—"

Slocum held up a hand. "I'm not dead, remember?" he offered, hoping to stave off any further tirade.

"You could'a been, Slocum! You could'a been, real easy!" MacCorkendale's eyes were bugged out, and his nose was ruddy. Slocum figured he'd been spending his day in a bourbon bottle. Then again, considering Helga, maybe it had been a bottle of schnapps.

In any case, he was clearly inebriated. It was a good thing it was dark. Otherwise, he might have done something really stupid, like round up his hands and ride down to Pablo Valdez's place with mischief on his mind.

Which was exactly what Slocum was trying to prevent.

"Sit down, Ralph," Slocum said. It was more on the order of a command than an invitation.

MacCorkendale didn't seem to notice, though. At least, he took no umbrage and sat down in a chair next to the door, his elbows on his knees.

"Now listen, Ralph," Slocum began. "Don't go off half-cocked on me. I don't even know who it was took a shot at me. Could'a been anybody."

MacCorkendale started to break in, to say something, but Slocum quickly said, "I know what you're thinkin', Ralph. But Jorgé Rodriguez wouldn't shoot from heavy cover like that. And he sure as hell wouldn't leave without making sure than his man was sure and certain dead. And as far as you've told me, Valdez has only hired on Jorgé Rodriguez, no one else."

MacCorkendale pursed his lips and narrowed his eyes, deep in thought. Finally, he said, "Guess we'll give 'em the benefit of the doubt. This time. But it if happens again, I'm gonna—"

Slocum waved his hand. "If it happens again, I won't care what you do, because I'll be dead."

MacCorkendale seemed to get a kick out of Slocum's gallows humor, or at least Slocum thought he heard him chuckle. And was saved from asking him about it when Helga burst into the room, bearing a tray.

"What you do here, Herr MacCorkendale?" she asked, eyebrows raised. "I think you are in parlor, getting drunk!"

MacCorkendale stood up, stared at her for a long moment, and then said, "If you insist, my dear."

He left, his steps down the hall much more measured than his clip-clop gait when he'd come up. Slocum didn't ask questions. He figured it wasn't his business if Ralph and Helga weren't getting along.

But Helga must have read his mind—or at least his face—because she said, "You are right to leave it alone, Herr Slocum." She set her tray down on the bureau.

"It's just Slocum, ma'am. No *Herr* to it."

She moved to his side. "*Ja, ja . . . Sitzen Sie* up, Herr Slocum. I am sorry. Slocum."

They worked until he was nearly upright and Helga had all the pillows behind him, and he couldn't help but notice that she had fine-textured, clear, creamy skin, and that she was pretty. Damned pretty, in fact, with that cornsilk hair all done up in old-country braids. He had a sudden urge to pull the secret pin that held it all up and watch it come tumbling down, but resisted it.

Light blue eyes and rosy cheeks floated above a full bosom, which filled out the front of her long white apron, and while she wasn't as slender as, say, Maria, there was flesh enough to hang onto.

Yesterday, he had let the idea that she was MacCorkendale's wife blur his vision of her, but now he was forced to really see her as she was.

As she placed the bed tray on his lap, he wondered if MacCorkendale knew what he had. "Thank you," he said as she lifted the cover off his supper tray.

It was chicken, with big, fluffy dumplings floating in a gravy thick with peas and chopped onions and corn and carrots.

He licked his lips. "Looks mighty good, ma'am!" he said, honestly eager.

She smiled for him and muttered, "*Dank*, Slocum. I bring buttermilk also," she said, producing a glass from God knows where and placing it on the tray beside his enormous bowl of chicken and dumplings.

"*Und* if you are still hungry when you finish that," she said, reaching across him to pull a smaller napkin from a smaller plate, "There is *Apfel* pie."

He grinned. "Apple pie? My favorite! Mrs. MacCorkendale, ma'am, it's a real pleasure to be shot up in your house."

She laughed then, and he quickly said, "Well, you know what I mean . . ." And then he chuckled, too.

She stood erect then, accidentally brushing her breast against Slocum's arm. He smiled because it felt so firm and round and good, but she flushed hotly and appeared flustered.

"I go now," she said, staring at the floor, and she practically ran from the room.

And Slocum thought, *Now, wasn't* that *interesting?*

On the other side of the border, Pablo Valdez and Jorgé Rodriguez were both fuming. Before them stood Pepé Mondragon, one of Valdez's vaqueros, who had just bragged about having shot a gringo on a spotted horse earlier in the day. One of MacCorkendale's hirelings no doubt, he had added.

"Idiot!" Jorgé had exploded, and then quickly explained to his employer just exactly who that man on the Appaloosa had been.

"Idiot!" repeated Valdez, much to Pepé Mondragon's dismay. Then he turned to Jorgé. "Why is he an idiot?"

"Because, Pablo, as I have told you—if you kill this Slocum, MacCorkendale will only call in more men. Many, many men to take Slocum's place. Do you wish to go to war over a few head of cattle?"

Valdez turned his attention back to Pepé. "Get out!" he commanded.

Pepé did.

"Those cattle are mine, Jorgé."

"So you have said many times, Pablo."

"The moment they cross the border, they are mine," Valdez went on. Jorgé thought he sounded more like he was trying to convince himself of it with every repetition.

"That, you have said many times, too, Pablo."

Valdez fell into silence, and Jorgé knew better than to try to coax him out of it. He simply went to the little bar in Valdez's study, picked up the decanter, and poured himself a fresh whiskey.

It was very dark outside, which was the only thing preventing him from riding out this minute and going to look for Slocum. Or at least, Slocum's body. However, he had a hard time convincing himself that a stinking little hand such as Pepé Mondragon had brought down the mighty Slocum. There was no justice to it, not even any symmetry.

No, despite Pepé's claim to a clean kill, he still believed Slocum was alive. He'd go in the morning and look—and he'd take that little pip-squeak with him—but he doubted he'd find a thing.

Except, possibly, trouble. But this was nothing new to Jorgé. Trouble, he could handle.

He took a sip of his whiskey, then turned back toward Valdez. "I will ride out in the morning," he announced. "I'll take Pepé with me."

Valdez's head jerked, as if he had been awakened from a dream. "What? Pepé who?"

"Pepé Mondragon. I will take him with me when I look for Slocum tomorrow."

"Ah," said Valdez. "Very good. Very good. Leave me now, Jorgé."

"As you wish, *patrón*," Jorgé said, and threw back the last of his whiskey. It was too good to waste.

In Jaguar Hole, Maria was throwing out the last of her customers. Two o'clock, and no Slocum.

She hoped he was well, that no harm had come to him. And then she shook her head and smiled to herself. What harm could come to a man such as Slocum? He was invincible, was he not?

At least, last night he had been in her bed. He hadn't been moving very much—mostly snoring, as a matter of fact—but he had been there, and warm, and when she had climbed atop him, he had grown hard even in his drunken state, and she had been able to mount him.

But then, after she had taken her pleasure, she had felt a little like a rapist must feel. She knew it was silly. She knew Slocum would have been the first to approve of such an act on her part. But still, she much preferred him conscious.

The last man went out the batwings, and Maria closed the bigger, solid doors behind him and locked them. Turning around, she leaned back on them, crossed her arms, and sighed.

5

The sun had barely cleared the horizon when Jorgé set out on his black Paso Fino for the long canyon. At his side trotted a nice little pinto gelding, with Pepé Mondragon aboard.

Jorgé could tell that Pepé was none to happy about this little trip, and in fact, feared he would not return from it alive. This was evidenced by his constant mumbling and fondling of his crucifix and his occasional, hopeful, skyward glances.

Pepé's God was going to save him today, Jorgé thought. Unless, of course, they rode up on Slocum's dead body. To tell the truth, he didn't know what he'd do if that were the case.

Kill Pepé? Probably, or at least make him wish he was dead. But for the moment, anyway, Pepé was in no immediate danger.

The canyon opened up before them, and Jorgé rode right down the middle.

"Shouldn't we go up along the top, as I did yesterday?" Pepé asked sheepishly.

"No," said Jorgé. "What were you doin' up there, anyhow?"

"Looking for strays," Pepé replied, eyes on his saddle horn.

"And you just happened to see an hombre riding along, down here?"

"Sí, señor."

"How'd you know he was riding out to Valdez's?"

Pepé shrugged. "He just looked like a pistolero, that is all."

Jorgé ground his teeth. Just *looked* like a gunman. He said nothing, though.

A scant hour later, right at the center of the long canyon, Pepé reined in his horse. Twisting in his saddle, he pointed to a place high atop the canyon walls. "I was there. He fell somewhere around here."

"Bet that spotted horse of his didn't run off, did it?"

Pepé shook his head.

"Didn't think so. You see that horse anywhere?"

"No."

Jorgé grunted and started what he was pretty damned sure would be a fruitless search for Slocum's body.

Fifteen minutes later, he found a patch of flattened weeds and dried blood.

"Pepé!" he shouted. "He went down over here!"

"Is he dead?" Pepé replied, a little too hopefully. The idiot.

"No, Pepé, and you'd better thank Our Lady of Guadalupe. Because if he had been, you'd have been next. *¿Verdad?"* Jorgé snarled.

Pepé had the good sense to cower in his saddle.

Jorgé was busy looking at the ground. A man had lain here for quite a while, to bend the brush so completely. And then he had gotten up, remounted, and ridden back the way he had come.

Slocum was alive, but he'd lost a good deal of blood. Had he headed for the ranch of MacCorkendale, or for town?

Town, Jorgé thought. Slocum had been sweet on Maria Anna Lopez.

But then, who wasn't? She only had eyes for Slocum, though, that lucky hombre!

He said, "Go back to the rancho, Pepé, and tell Señor Valdez that Slocum lives, and I have gone to speak with him."

Pepé nodded in the affirmative and turned his horse around. Without another word, he spurred his pinto toward home.

Maria was in the kitchen when she heard boots clomp in the doors and heard Diego say, *"Buenos días, Señor Rodriguez. Cerveza? Tequila?"*

But then Rodriguez answered, "Slocum."

Maria set aside the sopaipillas she was making and stepped out front. Dusting her hands on her apron, she said, "Jorgé Rodriguez? Is that you?"

He turned toward her. Again she was struck by how handsome he was. You would never expect him to be a hired gun. Well, perhaps some would—like Slocum, for instance—but she supposed it took one to know one. Jorgé was tall, narrow, and black-eyed, with long, narrow fingers that she thought were beautiful.

Not that they'd ever touched her. She had no time for men and the trouble they brought, excepting Slocum on those rare trips he made through Jaguar Hole. And now Slocum was bringing trouble, too. She did not like the tone of Jorgé's voice.

"What is it, Jorgé?" she asked. "What is wrong?"

"Buenos días, Señorita Maria," he said, gallantly bowing from the waist while he doffed his sombrero with a flourish. He rose again, grinning. "I am looking for Slocum. He is here?"

Her eyes narrowed with suspicion. "No. He is not. Why?"

"Then he has gone to that rancho of Señor MacCorkendale," Jorgé said with a shake of his head. *"Caramba,"* he hissed. "I cannot go there."

"Jorgé—?"

"He is hurt, Maria. One of Señor Valdez's men was a little too . . . eager."

She felt herself stiffen. "Hurt? How badly?"

"He is shot, Maria. That is all I know." Jorgé shrugged, but he still looked worried.

"Then you must go to the MacCorkendale rancho!" she said.

"No, MacCorkendale, he will shoot me on sight."

She looked around at the lunch crowd gathering, at Diego running plates from the kitchen to the tables. She couldn't leave, not now. There were more enchiladas to bake, sopaipillas to fry, beans to stir, rice to make . . .

Diego could handle it.

She said, "I will go, then," and began to untie her apron. "Diego," she shouted, "take over for a little while."

She had the apron all the way off and folded on the counter, and was just taking her first strides toward the door when Slocum walked in.

"¡Madre de Dios!" Jorgé cried behind her. "He lives still!"

Slocum looked pretty startled when Maria jumped into his arms, but he seemed happy about it. Never had she been so happy to see him! He was favoring one arm, though, and she carefully extricated herself from his grip.

"You are all right, my love?" she asked, then snapped her head to one side, toward a watching patron. "Eat your enchiladas, Franklin, the floor show is later."

Franklin kept his eyes on his plate.

"Don't worry, baby," Slocum said, and gave her a one-armed hug around her shoulders. He gave Jorgé Rodriguez a serious look. "Jorgé, I think we need to have us a beer and a confab."

"Agreed, Slocum," Jorgé said, equally serious. "Diego!" he called. *"¡Dos cervezas, por favor!"*

"Well, why the hell'd you let him ride out of here?" MacCorkendale railed.

Helga held her ground, although her initial instinct was to run from him. As calmly as she could, she said, "What is it you expect I should do, Herr MacCorkendale? Wrestle him to the ground? He is the big, strong man!"

Just saying those two words—*big* and *strong*—out loud made her all wet between her legs. She had never had this reaction to any man before, not even Herr MacCorkendale, and it alternately frightened and thrilled her.

She crossed her arms over her bosom and said, "If he wishes to go, I can not stop him."

And she really wished that she could have. She had pleaded with him that his shoulder was not healed enough for him to travel, that the "Spanish poison," as she had dubbed the medicine Slocum had told her was put in his coffee, had not worked its way out of him yet, and a dozen other reasons. She had done everything but rip her blouse open to expose herself.

Now she was wishing that she had done just that.

What would it feel like to have a man like that—so, well, totally *male*—touch her on skin that only a husband touched? She shuddered, and her arms broke out in gooseflesh.

MacCorkendale said, "What the hell's wrong with you? You look all . . . flushed or somethin'."

"Ich weiss nicht," she said, ducking her head. Hot color was flooding into her cheeks, too. "I go back to kitchen now?"

"Yeah, yeah," said MacCorkendale, waving a dismissive hand. "I'll just go after him, that's all."

Helga turned. *"Nein,* he said you were not to follow him. That no one was to follow him."

"Are you joking with me?"

Joking? Why in God's name would she be joking? She said, "No, Herr MacCorkendale. Herr Slocum was very serious—very much in earnest—when he said it to me."

"And stop callin' me Herr MacCorkendale!"

"*Ja,* Herr MacCorkendale."

Suddenly, his arm shot out. He backhanded her, and she tumbled against the wall, then slid down to the floor. She landed with a thump, and it took her a second to realize what had happened.

MacCorkendale stood above her, shaking his fist. "Next time, remember, goddamn it!"

Her hand to her cheek, she nodded. "Yes. Ralph."

She pulled herself to her feet and faced him. There were finer men than Ralph MacCorkendale out there. There were smarter men, and kinder men. The only reason she had said yes to him, she remembered, was because her mother had always said she was too big and too ugly to ever get a husband.

"Herr MacCorkendale," she said softly but clearly, and with complete earnestness, "you will not again hit me. If you do, I will hit you back, and I am very strong. And if you make the same mistake a second time, I will poison your food. Do you understand what I say?"

He stood there, blinking in silent shock.

"Good," she said, and turned on her heel. The beets she was boiling for lunch should be ready to come off the stove.

"Sometimes I feel like I should just put a slug into him myself," Jorgé said, between sips of his cerveza.

"Save everybody a whole lot of trouble," Slocum agreed. Maria had left them momentarily to check on the kitchen. There was quite a crowd in Cantina Lopez for lunch, although not so big as the one last evening. "Don't suppose we could just string up a fence all down the border," Slocum said.

Jorgé barked out a laugh. "Very funny, amigo! I do not know where we could find the barbed wire!"

Slocum shrugged. He'd been serious about the fence. He said, "I do."

"Do what?"

"Know where we can get the wire."

"*¿Que?* You are meaning this?"

Slocum nodded.

"This I cannot believe!" said Jorgé. "You think you and I together could put up a fence this long?"

"I'm not opposed to a little manual labor," Slocum said, allowing his lips to quirk up into a smile. "I've done it before, won't kill me to do it again. And if it'll keep these two idiots from killin' each other, it'll be worth it." He paused to light the quirley he'd just rolled. "What you think, Jorgé?"

Jorgé shook his head. "For true? I think you are crazy, Slocum, as crazy as a bedbug in the locoweed, and that is very much crazy. But," he added, holding his arms out, hands palms up, "if you think there is a chance, I am willing to do some work with my hands." He leaned across the table. "You will provide the gloves and tools, no?" he asked with a wink.

Slocum laughed. "Don't worry, Jorgé. All I'll need from you is muscle."

"And you will never tell another man that Jorgé Rodriguez has helped you do this thing?"

"Word of honor."

Jorgé stuck out his hand. "Then we have a deal, my friend."

Slocum shook firmly, then said, "How many miles of fence you reckon we're talkin' about?"

"Eleven, maybe twelve."

Shit. Slocum had hoped it would be less. A lot less. But he supposed they wouldn't have to fence all of it. There would be natural boundaries here and there, places where the terrain prevented the cattle from crossing the border.

"I'll send for the wire this afternoon," he said. He hated the stuff, but there were times when it came in real handy. Like this one, for instance.

"How you think Valdez'll take to this idea?" he asked.

Jorgé rolled his eyes. "He will not take to it at all," he said with a shake of his head, "but I am past the caring. He is a man who will not listen to reason."

"I tell you, Jorgé," said Slocum, "those two stubborn peckerwoods could be brothers."

"True," replied Jorgé. "Very true."

6

That evening, Slocum was still congratulating himself on the sterling idea of a fence while he waited upstairs for Maria to toss the last lingerers out of Cantina Lopez, and listened to mariachi music coming up through the floorboards. He'd ordered twenty-four miles worth of barbed wire this afternoon—figuring on double-stringing it, and on Jorgé's estimate of the distance to be only slightly reliable—and it would be coming in on a freight wagon in a day or two.

Jorgé knew of a good-sized stand of pin oak out on Valdez's place and volunteered to supply the posts. Slocum figured they'd probably be fairly thin and stringy, but beggars couldn't be choosers. Besides, once he and Jorgé solved the problem and left, it'd be up to somebody else to maintain the fence.

He was satisfied.

Actually, he was overjoyed. It sure beat killing Jorgé—something he really didn't want to do—and God knows how many other men.

Or maybe getting killed himself.

As much as he figured MacCorkendale to be in the right, he still thought that MacCorkendale was a lunatic, sometimes. How he'd ever ended up with that pretty Helga of his was beyond Slocum.

Well, that got him to thinking about Helga, which he did for quite a while—and most happily—until Maria opened the door. He was so engrossed in imagining Helga's creamy, white breasts that he was almost shocked when the darkly beautiful and exotic Maria cocked a brow at him.

"Am I interrupting?" she asked.

"How could you possibly?" he said with a sheepish grin.

"You looked . . . as if you were meditating. Or in prayer."

"If I was," he said, grinning, "it was only that you'd hurry the hell up, darlin'."

She smiled seductively and sashayed closer.

He held out his arms.

Helga MacCorkendale couldn't sleep. She lay beside Herr MacCorkendale, whose snores indicated he was having no such trouble.

What was to become of this business with Slocum and Valdez? It seemed to her that her husband was intent on starting his own private war. And over something so silly as a few cows! Herr Valdez said they were his, because they had wandered onto Mexican soil, a part of which he happened to control.

Perhaps he was correct. Perhaps he had every right to take them for his own. Helga was not acquainted with the legalities of their situation, and so far as she knew, her husband had not consulted an attorney. Or even the sheriff. He had just shouted and carried on and grown most evil tempered, and then he had hired Slocum.

Mostly, it was Slocum for whom she feared.

Her mother had told her she should feel honored and very lucky that a man such as Herr MacCorkendale was interested in marrying her. Her mother had told her that love came in time, over the years, and not to worry her head about it.

Her mother had lied to her, she now realized.

She was, in fact, very unlucky that Herr MacCorkendale had taken a liking to her. And that he'd married her. And love hadn't come, even though it had been two interminable years.

All she was to him, she well knew, was a cook and housekeeper, and someone for him to occasionally use to fulfill his husbandly needs. Not that he had many. Once every couple of months, that was it.

Of course, he had built her the house she wanted, long ago when they were newly wed, but she sometimes wondered if he had a woman in town, someone he went to, to quench his desires. Men had more of those feelings than women, she had heard. And if he had more than she, they must need a great deal of fulfilling, indeed.

Never in her life had she experienced such a strong and immediate attraction to a man as she had to Slocum. It was completely carnal and physical, and it filled her with a yearning, burning lust. She feared that she would probably burn in hell for it.

But somehow, she found that she just didn't care.

She imagined his narrow hips and broad shoulders, the muscles that belled his arms, and all those scars—how she would like to ask him about those!—that covered his torso. And his voice, so baritone, so smooth, so . . . she didn't have a word for it, but she felt her own hand slip beneath her nightgown and slide between her legs.

To the sound of Herr MacCorkendale's snores, she began to pleasure herself. She did this often, but never before had she done it while thinking of a particular person, a real man that she had actually met.

Images of Slocum flashed through her mind, memories, real and imagined: the sight of him, the sound of him, how his skin felt, his scent.

She came so forcefully that she must have cried out, because Herr MacCorkendale sat bolt upright in the middle of a snore, and said, "What? What?"

She took a moment to gather herself, to get her breathing under control and to try to clear her head. And then, without turning toward him, she said, "You are dreaming, Herr MacCorkendale. Go back to sleep."

And then held her breath while he cursed and settled back in.

She didn't let herself relax until he started snoring once more.

When his snores became deep and rhythmic, she finally allowed herself a sly, secret, sleepy smile, and breathed, "Slocum."

Maria lay naked and sweating upon the rumpled sheets, on her side, one leg carelessly slung over Slocum's hip. He was drowsing. She smiled when the thought crossed her mind that she had worn him out. Well, she supposed three times in one night was a great deal to ask of any man, even one such as her Slocum.

Although she was hoping that he'd wake up and make it four.

But she did not disturb him. She didn't fully understand why he was in town this time, other than that Ralph MacCorkendale had hired him. She wasn't certain exactly what he'd been hired to do, but the fact that he was talking to Jorgé Rodriguez was interesting. MacCorkendale and that man Jorgé was working for, Pablo Valdez, had much bad blood between them.

Something about cattle.

She didn't pay much attention to the local gossip. Mostly, she was concerned with her family, with keeping her mother's head above water, with keeping her sister's children healthy and growing up right, and with praying that her ne'er-do-well brother-in-law had gotten himself killed over cards or a woman. Those things, in themselves, made a full enough life for her.

For anyone, she sometimes thought.

Slocum stirred a bit, and she held very still, watching him. The second time, he had taken her against the wall, and she had enjoyed that very much. She liked the feeling of being weightless, off the ground, of riding Slocum's beautiful cock with her legs wrapped tight around his waist and his hands on her backside, controlling her every move, her every nuance.

He excited her as no other man ever had. Or probably ever would.

He stirred again, and this time, opened one eye. She smiled at him. He smiled back.

She whispered, "Again, my love?"

A grin crawled across his face, and he said, "Some girls . . ."

She giggled, and he pulled her close and kissed her.

She felt his erection thumping against her belly, and she said, "This time, the table?"

He chuckled, and it vibrated through her. "Get across it, gal," he said.

She jumped from the bed and slid onto the cool wood. The window was beside her, and it let in a cool breeze that felt good on her skin.

He was there immediately, standing between her parted legs. She felt him nudging at the portal to her inner core, and smiled. "You don't have to knock, Slocum," she purred. "You are welcome to come in whenever you wish."

He hooked his elbows around her thighs and rammed into her with such force that it literally took her breath away. The next thing she knew, her knees were over his shoulders, he held her hips, and he drew her to receive his thrusts again and again.

She could do nothing but hang onto the sides of the table for dear life. Her pleasure rapidly approached its peak, fire raced through her veins in the heady, impossible, tactile joy of it.

Just as she toppled off the edge of the cliff, exploding like stars, she felt Slocum plunge into her with even more vigor, and her body responded with an unconscious clenching of her inner muscles. This only made her reaction even more rapturous and seemed to increase his pleasure, too.

He thrust into her, just three more strokes, and left her throbbing and shaking with the intensity of it. Still within her, he eased her legs down from his shoulders, then bent forward at the waist to kiss her, to rest his weight upon her torso while he gently cupped her breasts.

"Maria," he whispered, and kissed her again. "Maria."

Jorgé Rodriguez woke before the dawn and set out for the northeast part of the rancho with a wagon (with two of Señor Valdez's horses hitched to and pulling it, and his saddle horse tied behind), two days' worth of feed and water and food for himself, two saws, a posthole digger—for later—and an ax.

He arrived at his destination just as the sun was coming up, and he smiled. Many good trees were here, many good trees that he could chop down and turn into fence posts for barbed wire.

He knew they wouldn't be the best fence posts, but they would be good enough to get the job done, and this was all he was concerned about. This, and that someone might see him. Señor Valdez would not be very happy about him and Slocum building a fence and using his stand of pin oak to make the posts.

Not very happy?

He would be furious.

And from the stories Jorgé had heard, Señor Valdez's fury was something he did not wish to witness.

Sighing, he climbed down off the wagon, unhitched and

staked out the horses, reached for the saw, then changed his mind and picked up the ax instead. He'd just chop off some low branches, to start. There was no sense in going all out right away.

He'd work his way up to it.

He slung the ax over his shoulder and set off toward the trees, whistling.

7

Later that morning, while Jorgé was busy cutting fence posts and Slocum was riding out to the MacCorkendales' spread to await his wire—and break the news of his plan to MacCorkendale—the biweekly stage rolled into Jaguar Hole. Down from it climbed a single passenger, one Samantha Rollings.

She had heard that Slocum was headed down this way and had very boldly followed him. He'd spent the previous week with her over at Bisbee—the most pleasant week of her life, as a matter of fact—and she was determined to repeat the experience.

Samantha had worked for Miss Daisy up at the Regal Saloon, but that didn't make her a prostitute, no sir! Why, she figured you had to have that kind of, well, mind-set, to be in that sort of business. And even though she slept with men for money, she didn't have those kinds of sensibilities.

She couldn't help it if her daddy had left her and her mama, and then her mama had died, now could she? She'd just fallen into the business temporarily—well, three years ago, to be exact—until things looked up.

They had looked up considerably when the famous Slocum, his very own self—the one the men talked about in back rooms, the one in the dime novels—walked through the doors of the Regal Saloon and took a shine to her. For a whole week he'd stayed in town, practically living upstairs at Miss Daisy's—and in Samantha's room—and then he'd left. Just like that!

Nerve, that was what he had.

She'd spent a day being mad and listening to Miss Daisy tell her over and over that: (1) men didn't stay on, and (2) that men, especially men named Slocum, didn't stay on.

The next day Samantha had quit her job and climbed on a stage.

She was bound and determined that Slocum would at least spend some time with her—and by that, she meant some serious bedroom time—or that he'd marry her. Both, if possible.

That would sort of make her famous, too, wouldn't it?

Her hand tightened on her purse as the driver helped her down from the stage. She'd gone so far as to buy herself an engagement ring, which she'd tied into the corner of her hankie, then stuffed into her handbag. Precious cargo, that. It hadn't been a very expensive purchase—just a very slim silver band with three little turquoise stones—but it was enough. She didn't plan on giving Slocum any time to think about buying one for her.

She stood in front of the station for quite a while after the horses had been changed and the stagecoach had departed. And she was more than a little annoyed that Slocum hadn't magically shown up to greet her. So what if she hadn't told him she was coming!

He should have just *known* shouldn't he?

But she waited and waited, and finally, when she didn't see hide nor hair of either him or that stupid polka-dot horse of his, she picked up her bag and made her way to the hotel.

She figured to check in, ask a few questions, and if that

didn't pan out? Then she'd go across the road to the cantina to get herself a bite of lunch and inquire there.

"Rodriguez! What in the hell are you doing?"

Jorgé froze, mid-chop. Señor Valdez's voice boomed out, shaking the very trees, and Jorgé was almost afraid to turn and look at him.

But he did, and what he saw on Valdez's face was most terrible. Flanking him on horseback were Juan and Carlito, two of his toughest hands. Carlito was smiling a most unpleasant smile.

Jorgé let his ax drop to the ground and used it as a walking stick, leaning on it. *"Hola, Señor Valdez.* What in the world are you doing out here this morning, so far from your rancho?" he asked, smiling.

Act casual, Jorgé, he told himself. *You may talk your way out of this yet.*

But Señor Valdez did not appear as if he would be easily swayed. Again he demanded, "What are you doing out here, chopping my trees down? We have no need for firewood. And if we did," he added, "I have much less expensive help to cut it."

Jorgé took a deep breath. He supposed he would have to fess up sooner or later. He said, "Señor Valdez, I am cutting posts for your new fence."

Valdez's brow furrowed. "My new fence? I have ordered no such fence. I hate fences."

Jorgé shrugged. "So do I, *patrón,* so do I. But Slocum and I, we have spoken at much length. We agree that the only way to keep those damned steers of MacCorkendale's from invading your property is to string one up. A fence, I mean," he added when he saw Carlito's face brighten on his mention of stringing up something.

He would like to get Carlito out behind the barn, he thought. He probably would have that opportunity before he finished this job.

"No," said Valdez. "I do not approve."

"I was afraid of that, señor," admitted Jorgé.

"This is obvious. This is why you have sneaked out before the dawn, is it not?"

Jorgé didn't flinch. "Yes, it is. I had the feeling that you might not approve of the fence being built, but that once it was up, you would not have it torn down. I do not wish to see this dispute between you and MacCorkendale turn into a border war, Pablo. I do not wish to see your land occupied by troops instead of steers."

This stopped Valdez cold. At least he said nothing, and he actually appeared to be thinking it over. Jorgé hoped his thoughts were of the positive variety.

At last he spoke, and when he did, it was amazing. "All right, Jorgé," he said, counter to everything that Jorgé expected.

Jorgé congratulated himself on his persuasive powers while Valdez continued. "You have more experience with these things than I. We will try your way and see what happens. Carlito and Juan will stay and help you."

Carlito said, "But, *patrón*—"

"You will stay and assist," Valdez said firmly and reined his horse away. "For as long as you are needed."

"Yes, *patrón*," Juan muttered, shrugging.

Carlito looked daggers at Jorgé.

Jorgé simply smiled back innocently and said, "Welcome, amigos. Saw or ax?"

Slocum rode into the MacCorkendales' yard and tied Concho to the rail out front. He wasn't looking forward to this, but it had to be done sooner or later. He figured that MacCorkendale would likely explode with anger when he heard the news about the fence, but he was going to have to hear it.

Slocum just hoped MacCorkendale wouldn't blow himself—or Slocum—into the next world.

He climbed the steps to the porch, then rapped on the door.

Helga answered it. She didn't say hello or how are you. She didn't say anything. Her mouth dropped open, her pretty face turned red as a sunset, and she just stood there, hands over her breasts.

Slocum was a little flummoxed by this odd welcome, but finally said, "Morning, Mrs. MacCorkendale. Is the mister around?"

Helga opened her mouth as if to speak, then abruptly fell straight down to the ground.

Slocum blinked a couple of times, then bent down to her. "Mrs. MacCorkendale? Helga?" Then he looked back into the dark house and hollered, "Ralph! Hey, Ralph, you in there?"

A voice carried down the stairs. "That you, Slocum? Where in the hell you been? Me and Helga half expected you to come back for supper last night." MacCorkendale's boot steps neared, each strike echoing overhead.

"Better get down here, Ralph," Slocum warned. "Helga's gone and had the vapors on me."

The tempo of MacCorkendale's step picked up as he started down the stairs. "What's that you say? Why I ain't heard that term since I left . . ." He took one look at Helga on the floor, then vaulted down the last four steps. "Helga!"

He shoved Slocum out of the way and began patting Helga's face and hands. "Helga? Helga, honey, don't you go and die on me, now!"

Slocum picked himself up, then found his hat, which he tossed to the hall tree. Once he regained his composure, he said, "Ralph?"

MacCorkendale didn't even look up, just went on rubbing her wrists and imploring her not to die.

Again, Slocum said, "Jesus, Ralph! Don't be such an old woman. Go find her a wet cloth."

"A wet cloth," MacCorkendale muttered as he climbed

to his feet. "Of course. A wet cloth." He sprinted toward the rear of the house, leaving Helga to lie on the hallway floor in something of a heap.

Slocum muttered, "Shit, Ralph," then picked her up and carried her into the parlor, where he put her down on a small leather sofa between potted palms. MacCorkendale came in directly, carrying a wet dishcloth, which he applied to Helga's temples and throat.

She came round almost immediately.

Blinking, she looked around the room, took in her husband and Slocum, and then looked terribly flustered. "Excuse me, Herr Slocum, Herr MacCorkendale!" she said, then covered her face with her hands. Between her palms, she added, "I am very sorry."

"There, there, honey," MacCorkendale offered fairly lamely for somebody who'd been as concerned as he'd been a couple minutes ago. What was going on with him, anyway? He was a different man when his wife was conscious than when she was out cold.

Slocum gave a quick shake to his head. It didn't matter. Right now, he just wanted to talk to MacCorkendale. "Ralph?" he said.

"What?" Ralph looked anxious for an excuse to get rid of his wife, now that he was sure she was going to live.

"Maybe Helga'd like to go on upstairs and lie down?" Slocum said.

"Oh! Good idea!" said MacCorkendale and piloted the still unsettled woman off the sofa and to the bottom of the stairs. "Go on, now, Helga," Slocum heard him say. "Go and lie down." And then he heard the light tap of Helga's feet as she slowly climbed the steps.

MacCorkendale came back in the parlor, looking relieved.

"You let her go up alone?" Slocum asked, thinking to shame MacCorkendale into some sort of gentlemanly behavior.

It didn't work, though. MacCorkendale just sat down in his big easy chair, waved a hand, and—despite his earlier almost maniacal concern for his wife—said, "Oh, she'll be all right. Probably, it's the heat what got to her. Her folks come from the old country, y'know. It don't get hot over there, not like it does out this way."

Slocum decided to let it go. He had bigger fish to fry.

He slid into a chair opposite MacCorkendale's, propped up his boots, and said, "Ralph, I need to talk to you."

"Talk all you want, Slocum. It's free."

Slocum didn't smile at MacCorkendale's little attempt at a joke. He just went right to the point. "Ralph, me and Jorgé Rodriguez had us a long confab yesterday. There's only one way we can see to keep you and Valdez from rippin' each other's throats out, and that's a fence."

MacCorkendale's eyebrows shot up, and his face turned red. "A *what*?"

"A fence," Slocum repeated. "You heard me. Valdez is springin' for the posts, and you're buyin' the wire."

MacCorkendale started to interrupt, but Slocum cut him off quickly, saying, "It's already ordered. Now, me and Jorgé'll string it up, and we figure that'll take care of your steers crossin' the border. Mostly. You'll need to look after it after I'm gone. Send somebody out to ride it once a week or so. You know."

"I hate fences! I never had a place with a fence on it in my life!" MacCorkendale's face was not one iota less red than it had been before Slocum's speech.

"You've got a corral," Slocum offered.

"That's different!" MacCorkendale snapped.

Slocum took a breath. "No, it ain't, Ralph. You want to keep your saddle horses in one place, you fence 'em. Same for the damned cows. And it's not even a fence that goes all the way around anything!"

"No fences!"

"It's just a barrier, that's all. Jesus H!"

MacCorkendale was silent, and so was Slocum, mainly because he figured the next thing he'd do would be brain the man. Talk about stubborn!

Finally, a little of the crimson drained from MacCorkendale's face, and he asked, "Valdez gonna have his men patrolin' this thing, too?"

Slocum had no idea, but he said, "Far as I know."

MacCorkendale shook his head sadly. "A damned shame, that's what it is. Why, when his cows wander north, my boys just shoo 'em back south, over the border. Don't know why he can't just do me the same courtesy."

"Good question, Ralph," Slocum said. It looked like MacCorkendale was going to okay this little experiment after all, and Slocum wasn't going to press his luck.

"Gettin' dark," MacCorkendale said, looking out the window. "You stayin'?"

"Reckon so," replied Slocum. "That is, if your missus don't mind. Maybe you want to look in on her?"

"She'd better not mind," MacCorkendale said. He was still staring out the window. "And I don't feel like climbin' them stairs again."

Slocum unfolded himself from his chair. "Well, I'll go put my horse up, then."

"You do that," came the muttered response.

8

Having learned nothing of Slocum's whereabouts at the hotel, Samantha freshened up, checked her hair, pinched her cheeks, and locked her room behind her. She headed down the stairs and outside, crossing the dusty street to Cantina Lopez.

Her purpose was twofold: she was as hungry as a starved wolverine, and Cantina Lopez also looked to be the only restaurant in town. If anybody would know anything about Slocum, the people there would.

When she walked in out of the late afternoon's glare, she realized she was the only female in the place. This didn't stop her, though. She stuck her nose up in the air, walked straight to an empty table, and sat down, her back to the wall, her face toward the bar.

She scanned the crowd and didn't see him. She did, however, see a knot of men in the corner who had all turned to look at her, and several standing at the bar. She also saw a short Mexican man rounding the bar and heading toward her.

"Greetings, señorita," he said, smiling. "How may I serve you?"

"I'd like some lunch, please," she said.

"The menu, she is there," the man said, pointing to a chalkboard behind the bar.

She noted that all they had was Mex food, but she ordered anyway. You couldn't trust Mex food, in her experience. Sometimes it was fine, and sometimes it would send you to the shitter for three solid days. She asked the man to have it seasoned as lightly as possible.

Before he left the table, she said, "Have you by chance seen a man, a big man, in the last few days? He's American, called Slocum."

The little man nodded enthusiastically, "Oh, *sí* Señor Slocum! Yes, he is here often."

Success at last. Samantha allowed herself a smile. That ring was as good as on her finger!

"Will he be in tonight, do you think, Señor . . . ?"

"Diego, just Diego," he replied. "And maybe, maybe not. I think it is most probably too late. He has stayed the night with the MacCorkendales."

"The MacCorkendales?"

"His employers. He will likely be back tomorrow, maybe the next day."

"Thank you, Diego," Samantha said.

"Sí," he said with a little bow. "I get your food now." And then, when he was halfway back to the kitchen, he turned and said, "Maria, she will be here in a half hour. If anyone knows of Slocum's plans, it will be she."

He turned and disappeared through the kitchen door, leaving Samantha to wonder just who the hell this Maria was!

Jorgé Rodriguez—Mexico's answer to Wild Bill Hickok, presently employed by Pablo Valdez as a hired killer, and a man of murky and ruthless reputation—sat on the ground before a small blaze, idly tossing small twigs toward the coffeepot.

"I do not understand you," Carlito said. "You were hired by Señor Valdez for your skills with a gun, not with an ax."

"I explained that before," Jorgé said through clenched teeth. "And I am not going to do it again."

"That is right, Carlito," Juan said, and then he hissed, "Please, for my sake and yours, do not push him."

Jorgé heard Juan's comment but did not acknowledge it. Fear could be a healthy thing.

But Carlito wasn't done. "Blisters!" He held up his hands for all to see. "I have blisters on my hands!"

Carlito had been bitching about the fence all day—about cutting the posts, about the building of it, and how he was above all this—and Jorgé was close to the edge. He turned toward Carlito and snapped, "Just be glad you are alive to feel the pain, amigo." He did not smile when he said "amigo," either.

Juan hissed, "See, Carlito? Shut up! Here, I am making us a good stew." He stirred the pot again for emphasis. "There will be tortillas, too!"

Carlito just snorted, then turned away from them both.

Jorgé wanted to say that if Carlito hadn't been one of his employer's caballeros, he would have used his gun skills already, and happily. On Carlito.

But still, he said nothing except, "How soon for the dinner, Juan? My stomach is growling."

"Not long, señor," Juan replied. "Fifteen minutes, maybe."

"That's your problem, Juan," said Carlito, suddenly part of the conversation once more.

Juan looked over, and it appeared than even he was getting a little riled. "What? What is my problem, Carlito?"

"That 'señor,' " Carlito grumbled. "You do not work for him. He is not some god come down to earth. He is just a man, like you and me."

Juan's back stiffened visibly. "He is a great man, a man they write the books about. And now he works for Señor Valdez, just like we do. Except he is better. He deserves the respect."

Jorgé was getting to like Juan, but he already knew Carlito was the one to watch. There was nothing worse than a vaguero with an attitude, he thought, and gave his head a slight shake from side to side. *So proud, like a strutting cock. So damned stupid.*

"It's all right, Juan," he said, and gave the man a smile, although a brief one. He wanted to keep his eyes on Carlito. They all had to sleep here tonight, and Jorgé didn't want to wake up dead because of some fool with a grudge.

"If you feel this work is beneath you, Carlito," he said evenly, "then go back to the rancho. Juan and I will do just fine without you."

Obviously, Carlito hadn't been expecting this, because Jorgé watched conflicting thoughts rapidly run across his less-than-handsome face until he came to a decision.

"I will stay," he said.

It was apparent that he had decided that Señor Valdez's wrath at his disobedience would be far worse than a few blisters—and having to work under Jorgé for the next week or so.

Jorgé said, "Very good, Carlito. I am happy to have you."

All the men, Juan included, visibly relaxed. Jorgé was reasonably certain he would not be killed in his sleep. Tonight, anyway.

He turned his attention to the stew, which smelled quite appealing. Of course, after the physical labor he'd put in today, he imagined that a turd sandwich might smell good to him.

He was glad that the stew was made with rabbits, though, and some of the carrots, onions, potatoes, and seasonings he'd had in his saddlebags.

"Ready, Juan?" he asked.

"*Sí*, ready," came the answer.

Jorgé held out his plate.

• • •

Slocum sat at the center of the long dinner table, with Helga at its foot and MacCorkendale at its head. It was a table built for a dozen diners, so there were two empty chairs between Slocum and Helga, and two empty places between Slocum and MacCorkendale.

MacCorkendale had continued to act oddly all during the evening, and Slocum couldn't tell if it was the idea of a fence that was bothering him, or something else, something between him and Helga.

Because she was acting strangely, too.

She refused to make eye contact with MacCorkendale, and with Slocum as well. Every time he spoke to her, she colored hotly and answered the floor, not him, in short, monosyllabic sentences.

Well, if Helga and Ralph weren't getting along right now, he guessed it was no skin off his nose. At least the grub was good.

Helga had cooked up something she called Wiener schnitzel, and served it along with new potatoes, swimming in some kind of butter sauce, sauerkraut, and fresh-baked bread. He wasn't too crazy about the kraut, but the Wiener schnitzel and potatoes and bread sure hit the spot.

He noticed that MacCorkendale appeared to be put off by all of it except the potatoes. He stared at his fork, stared out the window, and tapped the table with his knife. Finally, when Slocum was about halfway through the meal, MacCorkendale spoke.

"I hired you to kill Rodriguez or Valdez or both," he said softly, although his fist clenched his fork tightly. "I didn't hire you to stretch a goddamn fence."

Slocum said, "I know, Ralph, but—"

MacCorkendale cut him off, suddenly shouting, "I didn't hire you to get all buddy-buddy with your big pal, Jorgé Rodriguez!"

Slocum sat silently for a moment, working his jaw muscles and grinding his teeth, and holding back his first instinct, which was to go pound Ralph MacCorkendale right through his fancy table.

At last, as calmly as he could, he said, "You're about that close to it, Ralph."

"Close to what?" the idiot went on, heedless. "Close to bankruptcy? Close to ruin?"

Slocum boomed out, "Close to gettin' your damn head caved in!"

Abruptly, MacCorkendale's visage turned from that of a roaring bear to a rabbit caught in a train's oncoming lantern glare. Helga tittered behind her hand, and MacCorkendale's glare returned, although this time it was focused on her.

Slocum spoke quickly, hoping to defuse the situation. "I told you, Ralph," he said, "this fence is a simple thing, and it's gonna fix a world of worries. You'll just have to trust me on it. Nobody has to get killed over the situation. Or even hurt, if we're lucky. Now, your lady has set us out a pretty good spread, so why don't we enjoy it and figure that in a few days, all your problems are gonna be taken care of."

And then for emphasis, he added, "See?" and took a big bite of schnitzel. "S'easy."

Helga blushed beet red.

And MacCorkendale didn't say a word. He just picked up his fork again and started moving the food around on his plate.

Why couldn't I have got stuck with Valdez and Jorgé with MacCorkendale? he wondered, as he heard the soft scrape of Helga's chair.

"I bring dessert now?" she said. She stared at the floor.

"That'd be fine," Slocum replied.

"Do what you want," grumbled MacCorkendale. "I don't care."

9

Samantha Rollings, who had waited an hour for Maria last night, to no avail, woke in her hotel room at a little past dawn. And her first thoughts were of Slocum. And the silver ring tied into her hankie.

And then she remembered Maria and got mad all over again.

She got up, got dressed, fixed her hair, and locked her room behind her. But before she set out for the cantina, she untied the little ring and slipped it onto her finger.

She smiled.

She was ready to meet this Maria, whoever she was.

Her nose in the air, her expression haughty, she walked downstairs and out into the breaking morning.

Helga MacCorkendale had been up since dawn. Well, if she wanted to be truthful about it, she had been awake most of the night, tossing and turning while her husband snored beside her.

Why had Slocum come here, to spend the night just a few feet down the hall? Didn't he know she ached for him, that she had wanted to touch herself all night long so badly that she had practically ground her teeth down to nubs?

How could he be so cruel? How could he be so unfeeling to one who lusted after him so strongly?

She didn't love him. She barely knew him. But her want for him was so strong that she was certain it was written all over her every motion, her every expression, that it drifted on her every word, even those unspoken.

She did not understand.

She did not care.

She simply wanted him to go, to let her life go back to its same old drabness and emptiness. That, she was accustomed to. This passion, this uncaring, wild-feeling passion, she was not.

She heard boots on the stairs. They were not MacCorkendale's footfalls. She tried her best to ignore them and busied herself with her cooking: oatmeal, steamed fruits, and eggs.

"Well, somebody's up, anyhow," Slocum said, from behind her. "I was beginnin' to wonder!"

She took a deep breath before she turned toward him. She still couldn't keep the smile from her face, though. "*Guten Morgen, Herr Slocum,*" she said, and felt her knees bend in a little curtsy.

And then she felt herself do something else, something far more terrible. She took a step forward, stood on her tiptoes, flung her arms around his neck, and kissed him right on the mouth!

When Helga flung herself at him, Slocum was taken completely off guard. He returned the kiss—more out of habit than thought—and then realized what he was doing—with the boss's wife!—and broke it off.

Perplexed, he held her by the shoulders, at arm's length, and said, "Helga?"

Damned if she didn't burst into tears!

He guided her to the kitchen table and sat her down,

then pulled out the opposite chair for himself. And then he waited.

At last, in a small, trembling voice, she said, "I am so sorry, *Herr* Slocum. I didn't . . . I didn't . . . I would be most pleased if you would not tell my husband of this."

"That's fine, Helga," he said quickly but gently. "He ain't gonna hear nothin' from me." That was for certain sure, at least. But why the hell had she latched onto him in the first place? Slocum wondered. "Are things not goin' so good between you and the mister?"

She looked up, and right away Slocum knew she wasn't going to give any further explanation. Her face was closed up tight as a clamshell. And the only words that came out of her mouth were, "Ach! Breakfast!" She hurriedly got up and took two quick steps to the stove, where she alternately stirred things or moved them off the burners.

"What? Are we eatin' in the kitchen now?" came MacCorkendale's voice, and Slocum looked toward it. MacCorkendale was standing in the doorway, slouched against its frame. He didn't appear to be in the best mood.

At the stove, Helga froze, her back to her husband.

Slocum picked up the conversation for her, though. "No, Ralph," he said. "I just came in to bother your wife with a little small talk and see what she was servin'. Soon as I grab some breakfast, I'm off to see how Jorgé's comin' with those fence posts. Wire won't be in for a day or two."

Ralph frowned at the mention of the fence but said nothing about it. He just said, "Fine. I'll be in the office, Helga," and turned on his heel.

"*Ja* Herr MacCorkendale," she replied softly, without turning around. MacCorkendale didn't notice. He was gone already.

And Slocum could see that she wanted him out of there, too. Whatever reasons she'd had for kissing him, they'd have to remain her own.

Too bad, really. He'd actually enjoyed it, brief as it had been.

He pushed back from the table and said, "I'll be in the parlor, Helga."

"*Ja*, Herr Slocum," she said. And kept her back to him.

Women, he thought. *Who the hell knows what goes through their minds, anyhow?*

Sitting at a rear table at Cantina Lopez, a plate of steaming huevos rancheros in front of her, Samantha Rollings ground her teeth as she watched Maria—at least, she thought it must be Maria, because she was the only other woman she'd seen in the place thus far—moving back and forth in the kitchen.

She caught the waiter's sleeve before he could get away, and asked, "Diego, is that the Maria you told me about yesterday? The one who might know where I can find Slocum?"

"*Sí*, señorita," he said. "You wish me to tell her you are here?"

Samantha played with the little silver ring on her left hand for a moment. "Yes," she said at last. "I do wish it."

She'd find out what was going on, by God!

Actually, she already had a pretty good idea, judging from the glimpses she'd had of Maria. That Slocum was no better than a tomcat in rut! If tomcats ever came into rut, anyway. She didn't know.

The eggs were still sitting before her, untouched, when Maria came out of the kitchen and walked up to her table, smiling.

"Good morning, miss," she said in a voice that Samantha would have said was polite and beguiling, had she been in her right mind.

But seeing that she wasn't, she heard a voice full of nothing but raw sex, the voice of a barn cat in heat, the voice of a yowling siren who was trying to steal her man.

"Do you know Slocum?" she asked, straight out.

"Yes, I know him," Maria replied and cocked her head curiously. "You are a friend?"

Samantha snorted. "I should say so." She fingered the ring again. "Could you tell me where I might find him?"

Maria's eyes narrowed slightly, but she said, "Certainly. He is probably at the rancho of Señor MacCorkendale. That is about eight miles east of town. I'm certain they would rent you a buggy at the livery, if you are in a hurry to talk to him. Or you can wait in town. I expect him tonight."

She expected him tonight? For some reason, this simple statement nearly threw Samantha into a fit. But she didn't give in to it. Not now. Not yet, anyway. She forced a smile and said, "I shall wait in town, then."

Maria bowed her head and said, "Very well, miss," then seemed to notice Samantha's untouched plate. "You do not like my eggs? Perhaps they are too spicy? When Diego told me you were white, I did not use so much salsa."

"No," Samantha said, her voice clipped. She picked up her fork. "They're just fine." She cut herself a bite of egg and took it into her mouth. When she bit down, it was as if someone had shoveled a hot coal between her lips, and tears came to her eyes.

Maria smiled.

Damn her.

She said, "Let me get you another plate. With no salsa."

"Fine." The word came out forced and hoarse and was immediately followed by the intake of a half a glass of water.

Maria slid the plate away and carried it off, and a few minutes later the waiter, Diego, brought her another plate of eggs—this time, with no salsa—with two slices of buttered toast and a little pot of sweet jelly of some sort.

"Better," she admitted.

Diego said, *"Bueno, señorita,"* and went back to the kitchen.

The girl was nice enough, Samantha had to admit, and she was a pretty good cook, too, if the eggs were an example. But that didn't mean she liked her. She didn't, not one bit.

She was far too pretty, for one thing. Far too . . . sultry, that was it. Back at the Regal, at Miss Daisy's, there had been a few Mexican girls working. But they hadn't been anything like this Maria. They'd been short and pudgy, and mostly as plain as a mud fence.

Maria was practically glamorous, and in a little dump of a town like this!

Not only did Samantha not like Maria, she thought she might very easily hate her.

She gave the ring on her finger a last turn, then finished her eggs. Tossing a few coins on the table, she walked out rather haughtily and made a point of not looking toward the kitchen.

She'd find somewhere else to eat lunch.

Slocum rode south, to the border or thereabouts, and then turned Concho west, toward the place Jorgé had said the stand of wood was. He spotted it a long way off, and when he rode closer, he saw that Jorgé had some help: two men—just dots of moving color, really—back in the copse of trees.

Had Valdez given him and Jorgé the loan of a couple of hands? He'd have to tell MacCorkendale. Maybe it would shame him into doing likewise.

"Hello the camp!" Slocum shouted as he rode up.

Jorgé was just coming up from the little woods, fence posts balanced on his shoulders. "Greetings yourself, amigo!" he called back. He deposited the posts in the nearly full wagon bed as Slocum rode up to it and dismounted.

"You boys have done yourself a mite of work!" Slocum said.

Jorgé nodded. "Valdez followed me out yesterday, and I had to . . . come clean with him, no?"

Slocum grinned. "How'd he take it? You cuttin' the posts from his wood, I mean."

"As well as can be expected, I think," Jorgé said. "He left me two men to help." He pulled a canteen from under the wagon's seat, had a long drink, and shrugged. "They are not much help—well, Juan is the best of the two—but they are better than nothing."

"Any help's a good thing," Slocum said and pulled out his fixings pouch.

"*Sí* it is," Jorgé admitted, and slouched down in the shade of the wagon. He looked up at Slocum and added, "And MacCorkendale? How did he take the news?"

Slocum finished up rolling his quirley and stuck it between his lips. "Fair," he said as he struck a match, then lit the smoke. "There's somethin' weird goin' on up there."

"At the MacCorkendale ranchero?"

"Yeah. MacCorkendale acts like he's got a poker up his butt most of the time, and this morning, his wife kissed me."

Jorgé looked at him curiously, waiting for him to go on.

"Well, she did!" Slocum added. "I don't know why. Hell, I was only lookin' at her cook pots."

"I must remember this technique."

"Oh, very funny, Jorgé," Slocum grumbled. "You oughta go on the stage, you know that?"

Jorgé stood up. "Yes, I know. And there is one leaving at noon, no?"

"Smart-ass," said Slocum.

"Yes, amigo," Jorgé said, smiling, and handed Slocum an ax. "Let us go do some damage to the trees of Señor Valdez."

Slocum ground out his smoke and hoisted the ax over his shoulder. "Someday, Jorgé . . ." he grumbled.

Jorgé slapped him on the back. "Someday never comes, my friend."

Together, they walked down toward the trees.

Jorgé whistled.

10

Samantha waited the whole morning, staring out her window at the vacant street and thinking evil thoughts.

She was able to get a bite of lunch at the hotel's little restaurant, although the waiter there suggested she eat at Cantina Lopez. When she gave him a dirty look, he'd seated her at a table, then served her an abominable lunch: dry roast beef on stale bread, a horrible, gigantic limp pickle, and for dessert, an orange so wizened and puckered and discolored that she couldn't bring herself to touch it, let alone eat it.

When she complained, he'd said, "Not my fault, miss. I told you to go to Cantina Lopez if you wanted *good* food, but you wouldn't listen, you had to be stubborn . . ."

Against her better instincts, she paid for the meal, though she left most of it on her plate. Then she had gone directly back upstairs and shut herself in her room again.

It was hot and stuffy, made no more bearable by the open window, but at least she could keep her eyes on the cantina from there.

Her mood alternated between outrage and hurt. She was going to give Slocum an earful when he got back to town, all right!

But then she'd play with the ring she'd bought herself and felt bad, bad that Slocum had been seduced by that jezebel across the road, then bad that he had forgotten her and their time in Bisbee so quickly, and worse, that he'd forgotten her at all.

Which would make her mad all over again.

It was a bitter, relentless cycle, and she was powerless to stop it.

Maria was a very smart girl in the ways of men. After all, didn't she serve them liquor and food and scrape them off the floor? Hadn't she been doing it ever since she could remember?

And she also thought she was a fairly good judge of character in general.

She was.

She had pegged Samantha Rollings right off as one of Slocum's previous conquests. Maybe one who was just a little bit crazy. Although Maria was wild about Slocum, she also was levelheaded. She knew he was a man—and what a man!—but she also knew this meant something else. He was not perfect, and especially, he was not perfect where women were concerned. He could be taken in as easily as any of them.

Now, whether Samantha Rollings had taken in Slocum—she seemed to make a big point of drawing attention to that cheap ring on her finger—or whether she was just plain crazy, or something in between remained to be seen.

In any case, Maria intended to confront Slocum about it the second he walked through the door. She had enough to take care of without having to babysit Slocum's crazy former girlfriend.

The kitchen door opened in from the alley, and two giggling, small children ran in. *"Tía Maria! Tía Maria!"* the little girl cried. "Alberto took my dolly!"

Alberto looked far too angelic to have stolen anybody's

anything, but Maria turned to him, bent down, and said, "Alberto, is this true?"

Alberto, all of six, turned those big brown eyes on her and said, *"Sí, Tía Maria.* But not to be bad. I promise."

Consuela, his junior by only a year, folded her chubby arms across her chest and stared down her nose as if to say, *I told you so!* It was on occasions such as this that Maria was reminded of her sister, and more, her crazy brother-in-law. At least he was absent. At least he had left her sister. He'd probably gotten himself killed by now.

Live in hope, she thought.

"Then why?" she asked the boy.

He looked up with complete innocence and smiled at her. "To make her cry," he said.

Maria stood up, shaking her head. "Alberto, give it back. And don't take it again, all right?" She didn't know why it fell to her to discipline the *niños* half the time. She was not their mother. Although she reminded herself that their mother was undoubtedly drunk again, passed out on the childrens' grandmother's sofa.

Family could be a burden at times.

"Do I have to?" Alberto asked, his face practically wadding up with disappointment.

"Yes, you do. And if you do not, your sister will tell me, and I shall tell your grandmother."

Alberto's eyes grew wide. "I promise." Then his voice dropped to a whisper. "Don't tell Grandmama?" he asked. He looked frightened.

Maria held back a smile and said, "I won't, if you give back the doll and promise never to take it again, Alberto. *¿Verdad?"*

He looked down at the kitchen floor and tried to dig a sandal-clad toe into the wood. "It is under your bed, Consuela. Behind the stuffed horse."

Consuela tightened her grip on herself, shifting her arms upward. "It had better be there."

Maria knew that the threat of "Grandmother's wrath" was enough to keep poor Alberto from even telling a *slight* untruth, and she said, "It is, Consuela. Go and see."

The little girl stuck out her tongue at her brother and vanished out the door, leaving Alberto to his misery and Maria to comfort him.

"Would you like a sweet, Alberto?"

He nodded in the affirmative, and she lifted him up and sat him on the edge of the table. "All right, my fine little torero."

He smiled. He always smiled when she called him a bullfighter. He was small for his age.

In the drawer of the table, she rummaged for the paper bag of lemon drops she always kept, found it, and popped one into his eager mouth. His lips curled into a smile as he happily smacked on it.

"Ah, torero, you remind me of your father a little," she said, sighing. Paolo Alba had ridden into town one fine day, all talk and machismo and flash, and before she knew it, he had married her only sister. The boy was like his father in many ways: above all, in the delight he took in causing trouble, and the ease with which he escaped it.

And Paolo had finally escaped her sister by just riding out of town one day when Alberto was one and Consuela was a newborn. And he hadn't been back since. Conchita took her solace in the bottle and left most of the care of the children to whomever was handy, usually their mother. Who herself had a bad hip and probably couldn't have kept up with a lame old cow, let alone two fiesty, constantly squabbling grandchildren.

Well, such was life, Maria supposed. She needed to keep the cantina going. It supported far too many people. And she had been glad when she moved from her mother's house and into the room upstairs.

It was just one step farther away, but the room had been going to waste. Her father had let it out to strangers sometimes, when the hotel was full. Which happened perhaps once every one or two years, at the most. Jaguar Hole was not the most prosperous or commonly frequented of towns.

At last, his candy half finished, Alberto had sucked up enough attention to suit him, and he jumped down from his perch. A monkey, that one was! Why, even from the moment of his birth, he had been covered with fine, soft hair, the color of a raven's wing. It had all fallen out in days, but they all remembered it.

"Go now, torero," she said, smiling softly, then followed him to the door. She leaned out it, calling after him, "And leave your sister's things alone from now on! You hear me?"

Alberto scampered out into the street without even acknowledging her.

Just like his father. Both of them were, when you got right down to it.

Slocum piled the last of the load of fence posts on the wagon. Fence posts? They were a pretty ragged lot, these chunks of pin oak, but he figured they weren't going for looks so much as function.

Apparently, Jorgé agreed.

At least, he had loaded some pretty shabby posts himself. He had no idea what Juan and Carlito thought, except that Carlito wasn't any too happy with the whole operation.

Of course, Carlito hadn't said anything. He didn't need to. Waves of animosity fairly rolled off his back as he worked.

Slocum leaned against the wagon's shady side, took a pull off his canteen, then rolled himself a smoke. Carlito aside, what he couldn't figure out was why nobody had come up with this idea before.

Especially MacCorkendale. After all, he was the one losing his damned cows.

"*Hola,* Slocum," Jorgé said as he walked up, his arms

full of saws and axes. He tossed them up into the wagon seat, one at a time, then slouched next to Slocum. "I think we are done, no?" he asked as he ran a sleeve over his forehead.

"For today, anyhow."

"When does the wire come?"

Slocum exhaled a long plume of smoke. "I'm hopin' for tomorrow. Where you wanna start stringin'?"

"Good question, amigo. The land of Señor Valdez, it starts about a mile west. Señor MacCorkendale's land starts over there, right about where the horses are tethered."

Slocum nodded. "Okay, let's back up a half mile to the west, then. Split the difference."

Jorgé grinned. "My plan exactly. Slocum, we should start a business together. We would never argue."

Slocum returned the expression and added a chuckle. "Except maybe about what *kind* of business."

"Yes, you have maybe got me there," Jorgé admitted. "So, we start in the morning?"

"Yeah, guess we could start setting postholes even if the wire don't come in. They're freightin' it in from Bisbee."

"Bisbee?" Jorgé asked, arching one brow. "When was the last time you were there?"

Slocum shrugged. "'Bout a week ago. Maybe a couple'a days more."

Jorgé's face lit up. "Then you have spent time in the brothels there?"

"Yeah," Slocum replied, and took a last drag on his quirley before stamping it out underfoot. "This time I stayed up at . . . the Regal. Miss Daisy Thompson's place. Why?"

Jorgé began to laugh, then he slapped his thigh. "At Miss Daisy's? Slocum, the world is too small for such as you and I."

"Huh?"

"Two weeks ago, I stopped at Miss Daisy's, too! Ah,

and spent many an hour in the pleasant company of her girl Samantha."

Slocum stared at him. "This is gettin' spooky, Jorgé. I was with her just last week."

Jorgé laughed again. "You are not fooling me, Slocum? A little girl, only this high?" He held his hand just below shoulder level. "Red hair and blue eyes, with the body of an angel?"

"And the tenacity of a badger," Slocum added under his breath.

Jorgé heard though, and roared out a laugh.

"You're gettin' way too easy to please in your old age, Jorgé," Slocum said with a grin.

Jorgé replied, "No Slocum, just the opposite. Miss Samantha, she pleased me fine!"

Slocum slapped him on the shoulder. "Then may she please you again, amigo!" His gaze wandered back into the trees, where he could see Carlito and Juan, who were deep in conversation.

"What you suppose those two are up to?" he asked, eager to change the subject. Samantha had been pretty fair in the sack, but she was as loony as a Carolina lake at nesting time.

Jorgé followed his gaze. "Hard to tell with those two. Like I told you before, Juan, he is all right, I think. It is Carlito you will want to keep your eye on."

11

As it turned out, all four of the hapless fencers rode into Jaguar Hole that afternoon.

Jorgé kept the conversation—if it could be called that—going, but Slocum was the only one who participated, if marginally. Juan and Carlito rode several yards behind, leading the wagon horses, and kept their traps shut.

It was just past dusk when they rode up the main street—all right, the only street—and Slocum insisted they stop at the livery to see to the horses before they went up to the cantina.

Carlito grumbled some about this, but Jorgé laughed and said, "Just like the old times. The same old Slocum. Feeds his horse before he feeds himself!"

"You do the same thing, and you know it," Slocum chided.

Jorgé cocked his head briefly, then said, "*Sí*, I do. But it is difficult to tease myself, amigo. I would get mad and shoot myself, and then where would I be?"

Slocum threw a brush at him, and Jorgé laughed.

Juan and Carlito kept their silence and quietly tended their mounts, although Slocum noticed that Carlito slid him a quick look.

It was not friendly.

• • •

Samantha Rollings was still holding vigil at her window and saw the four men walking up the street from the livery.

Among them was Slocum! She'd know him anywhere with those broad shoulders and those slim hips, that animal grace with which he walked.

She paid no attention to the other men. Slocum was her only focus.

And when they went into the Cantina Lopez, she snatched her shawl from the bed and took off out the door.

She had to go back, from halfway down the stairs, when she remembered that she'd forgotten to lock her door.

Or even close it.

Slocum and his group had barely settled at a table at the edge of the room when a female voice—which didn't belong to Maria—boomed, "Slocum, *darlin'*!" And Samantha Rollings, of all people, came charging across the room at him, her arms outstretched.

Slocum was so taken aback that he could only sit there, staring, but not Jorgé. No, Jorgé fairly leapt to his feet, held out his arms, and cried, *"Querida!"*

Samantha stopped dead in her tracks only five feet from the table. "Jorgé?" she said, blinking.

He moved toward her. "Yes, my love, my darling! You have come to visit us? How sweet, how wonderful! How beautiful you look!"

He embraced her—a little too tightly, Slocum thought. At least he didn't recall her eyes bugging out that much. But there was no stopping Jorgé. Even the fact that she'd called out for Slocum in front of the whole cantina hadn't fazed him.

And then Slocum realized it: Jorgé was in love. With Samantha.

Which was a little like handing a four-year-old your nitroglycerine and a box of matches. Big trouble.

For Jorgé, anyway.

Nobody was speaking—nobody in the whole place, that was—and Slocum figured somebody had to save the day, and it looked like that somebody was him.

He stood up next to Jorgé, and said, "Why, Miss Samantha! Mighty nice to see you." There, that was passive enough, wasn't it?

But Samantha stood, frozen in place, while Jorgé continued to grin like a fool. Slocum expected a line of drool to start dripping from the corner of his mouth at any moment.

He slapped Jorgé on the back—more to bring him to his senses than anything else—and said, "Ain't you the lucky one? Miss Samantha came all the way down here, just to see you!"

Jorgé showed some signs of life, and Slocum quickly added, "Miss Samantha, why don't you have a seat between me and Jorgé, here?"

He quickly grabbed a vacant chair from another table and wrestled it into place between his and Jorgé's. But closer to Jorgé's than his.

Samantha had taken some possession of herself by that time. She embraced Jorgé warmly, although she eyed Slocum during most of it, then rounded him to take her chair.

She smiled across the table at Juan and Carlito, neither of whom could muster a smile, even for her. Slocum made the introductions.

Carlito, of all people, finally spoke. He pointed a finger straight at Samantha and said, "I know you from somewhere, I think."

Samantha said, "Oh, I just have one of those faces."

"No, no," Carlito insisted. "I think maybe we have met before."

Just in the nick of time, Diego appeared at the table with his order pad.

"Señores y señorita?" he said and poised his lead. "What can I bring you?"

• • •

Helga ate in silence as did Ralph, at the far end of the table.

She thought he was chewing with annoyance on his mind, although she could not be certain. He did everything with some annoyance lately, even more than he had in the beginning.

Of course, things between them had been much better than they were at present. Which wasn't to say they were good, just better. Anything was preferable to this: his protracted silences, his outbursts, and the fact that he had never loved her at all. To have known love, then lost it, would be better than this endless stretch of nothingness, of treading the endless ocean of time.

She pushed the peas on her plate to one side, then back again. She had kissed Slocum. She had thrown herself at him like some wanton hussy.

If her parents had known, they would have whipped her, then sent her to the milk shed to stay until the shame had fallen from her. But they didn't know, no one knew, and there was no one to punish her.

Except herself.

And she hadn't the strength.

But how wonderful that forbidden kiss had been! The taste of his lips, the broadness of his shoulders under her arms, the feel of him and the scent . . .

"No," she said, aloud.

MacCorkendale's head came up, and he glowered down the length of the table at her. "No, what?"

She cringed. "Nothing."

"You don't say 'no' for no reason, Helga."

She scrambled for an answer. "I was just thinking out loud, that is all."

"Thinking about what?"

Helga took a deep breath and scrambled to come up with something. "I was thinking that maybe I would change the kitchen curtains to red ones, and then I thought no, it will be too hot in there."

Miraculously, MacCorkendale simply said, "Oh," and resumed pushing his spoon around.

This place was so hot! Even now, sweat trickled down her back, down her nose, matted her hair. Why had she come to this place?

To be with your husband, she reminded herself. But why follow a husband who is not a husband?

Why stay with him at all?

But where could she go, and who would have her? Her mother had always said that no one would, and Helga believed her. She knew she could not go home. Even her parents didn't want her.

But Slocum . . . Could she go away with Slocum? He hadn't made a face of disgust when she'd . . . done what she'd done.

Maybe he would take pity on her, take her to a new place. Perhaps, along the way, he would make love to her. Once, just one single night in his arms, would be enough to last her a lifetime.

"Pardon me?" she said. Herr MacCorkendale had spoken while she was far away, deep in thought, imagining herself in another man's embrace. She flushed hotly, adding to her discomfort.

"What's wrong with you, anyhow?" he grumbled.

"I am sorry. I am not feeling very well lately."

"Whatever. See the doc, then. And pass me the butter."

Maria watched their table from the widow behind the bar. A very delicate thing, this situation, she thought. Slocum, this woman, Jorgé, and the other two. They were unsuited to sit at the same table. They were unsuited to dine in the same town, actually.

She didn't know exactly what was going on, but that

woman who had been pestering her about Slocum sat at their table, too, waiting for her dinner, with Jorgé's arm tight around her shoulders—and Slocum leaning as far away as possible. It seemed that whatever attraction the woman felt for Slocum was one-sided, then.

Still, it made her a little angry. She knew it shouldn't, but it did. She and that woman, they were as different as night and day—both in looks and in bearing. Had Slocum been involved with her at some time?

Maria shifted food from cooking pot or baking dish to plate without thinking about it. All she could think of was that woman stank of a place of soiled doves. There wasn't a smell, not exactly, but everything about her demeanor was, well, cheap.

Worse than cheap. She had come in asking questions and playing with that poor ring on her finger as if it meant something.

Maria sniffed. As if she could be fooled by a ploy so childish as that!

Still, it rankled. She called for Diego and sent him back out with their supper orders. She had planned to go herself but decided to give it a little more time before she threw herself into the brewing situation.

Whatever it was.

Slocum had best explain himself to her satisfaction, though, or he would not share her bed tonight! On this count, she was certain.

"Stop it," Samantha hissed as she pushed at him. Jorgé's arm had lain heavy on her shoulder ever since she'd sat down, Slocum had scooted his chair as far away as he could, and she was tired of it! Tired of being forcibly fondled by the wrong man and tired of Slocum being so near, yet so far.

Jorgé pulled his arm back just a hair and exclaimed, "*Que?* What is the problem, my love?"

She saw the expression of puzzlement on his face, the fool, but she had run out of patience—and mercy—at this point. She said, "Jorgé, I came to see Slocum."

His arm left her shoulders abruptly, and she felt a cooling slice of air for a moment. She also noticed Slocum edging even farther away.

She whirled toward him. *"Don't* you move another *inch*!" she demanded fiercely.

Her raised voice was barely noticed by the other patrons beyond their table. The tequila had started to flow.

"What'd you just say to me?" Slocum barked. He didn't much like being ordered around, and although he'd take more from a female than a man, he wasn't going to take this!

But Samantha, as usual, wasn't getting the message. She snapped, "You just plant your butt in that chair, *Mister* Slocum!"

"That's it," he muttered, and immediately shoved his chair back.

He grabbed Samantha by the arm, jerked her up after him, and headed toward the door, dragging her behind.

He had no more than stepped out onto the walk and said, "Godammit, Samantha!" when Jorgé came barreling out and ran right into them.

Samantha knew that Maria wouldn't be far behind, and she actually welcomed the confrontation. Get everything out in the open!

But Slocum quickly hissed, "Jorgé's in love with you. I'd take that to heart if I was you."

Jorgé made a grab for Samantha, pulled her back into his muscular chest protectively, and said, "What the hell you think you are doing, Slocum?"

More people streamed out the door behind them, probably hoping for a good fight, and along with them came Maria. Her arms were crossed over her chest, and the devil was in her eyes.

Quite suddenly, Samantha was actually frightened.

• • •

Slocum took a deep breath. This might cost him everything, but Samantha had pushed it, and now Jorgé had pushed it farther.

He said, "Jorgé, Samantha is yours. Always has been, in my mind."

Well, at least, *some* fella's besides his. Any fella's! And before Samantha had a chance to open her mouth—which he could tell she was just aching to—he added, "Everybody knows I came here to see Maria. Wouldn't have taken this job if I couldn't have seen her, too."

That part was more truth than convenient lie; he'd had another offer of work up in Montana but had decided on Jaguar Hole for the dark-eyed reason standing just a few feet away, tapping her toe.

He turned back toward the working girl Jorgé held against his chest. "Isn't that true, Samantha?"

For once, she was silent. At the wrong time.

"Isn't it?"

At long last, she gave a tiny snort and said, "Yes. Of course. My heart belongs to Jorgé."

"Then what is everybody so excited about?" asked Jorgé, his tone once again jovial. "Come, let us eat the fine meal Maria Anna Lopez has prepared."

The crowd moved back inside.

Jorgé pushed Samantha in ahead of him and whispered grimly, "We need to talk, amigo."

"Later," Slocum replied under his breath, then followed Jorgé inside.

What was taking Slocum so long? Maria paced the room, her blue silk robe trailing on the floorboards behind her, swishing around her ankles when she turned and paced back to the window again.

She knew he wasn't with that little tramp. She had watched Samantha go into the hotel with her own eyes, watched her light the lamp in her room, watched her sitting there, staring down at the street.

Apparently, Jorgé was with Slocum.

Wherever they were.

She had closed the cantina early for this? For an empty bed? For an absent Slocum?

Bah!

She slipped her feet into her sandals, cinched the waist tie of her robe, and went out the door and down the stairs in search of him.

Jorgé sat on a bale of straw at the stable, his head in his hands. Across from him stood Slocum, prepared for anything from a fistfight to the sounds of manly wailing.

When Jorgé finally looked up at him, he said, "*Es verdad.* I knew she could not have come here for me. She did not know I was here. I should kill you, amigo, but I have chopped many posts today, and I am tired."

"You can do it another time," Slocum replied.

Jorgé actually grinned. "Ah, you are funny, my friend. And maybe I will kill you. Or won't," he added with a shrug. "These things are hard to tell. Right now, I only wish to go to bed."

"Samantha's waitin'."

"Do not remind me." Jorgé stood up and stretched his arms. "Tonight, I think I sleep with the horses. Alone, except for my Zorro."

"You sure?"

"*Sí.* Unless there is room for three in that nice bed of Maria's?"

Slocum's eyes narrowed. "And just when did you see her bed, Jorgé?"

The man barked out a laugh and said, "You see? Now the boot, she is on the other foot."

Slocum grinned, and bit off his annoyance. Jorgé deserved to get one in, and Slocum let it go by. "All right, you old owlhoot. Me, I'm gonna hike back up to Maria's and hit the sack."

He left Jorgé laying out his blankets on a mound of straw in an empty stall.

Walking up the street in the quiet night, he couldn't help but do a little silent fuming about Samantha. Damn her anyway! Since when did a girl like that think she could just chase him down, appear in his life all over again, and . . .

He shook his head. He'd slept with her, all right. He'd had a good time. And he had paid her.

But now, it seemed as if he was paying for it twice over.

Maybe she was crazy! Yes, that was it. He couldn't imagine any sane whore pulling that little stunt she'd just pulled. What on earth could she have been thinking?

If she was thinking at all.

He doubted it.

He was ambling along, staring at the ground and muttering under his breath, when suddenly a pair of sandal-clad feet appeared in front of him. And stopped stock-still.

His gaze traveled from the sandals and up a long, dark stretch of fabric to Maria's face. Her hair hung down about her shoulders like a cowl.

He said, "Mad at me, baby?"

Maria said, "Should I be? Was there anything to it? To her intentions, I mean. Did you lead her to believe you wanted her here?"

"No. To all of it."

Maria regarded him in silence for a moment. Then, smiling softly, she said, "Come to bed, my poor Slocum. I have been waiting for you."

12

The next morning found Juan and Carlito up at dawn and checking out of the hotel shortly thereafter. Juan had been gone half the night, but Carlito was too proud to let him know that he'd noticed. They popped into the cantina, thinking to find Jorgé there, but only Maria stood behind the bar.

"You are early," she said. "We do not open for an hour."

"Pardon, señorita," said Juan, and tipped his hat.

"You have seen Jorgé Rodriguez today?" inquired Carlito somewhat churlishly. He wasn't about to move until she answered.

But she kept at her work, polishing glasses methodically. "No," she said, putting down the last shot glass and picking up a new one. The bar towel went to work. "Slocum says Jorgé slept in the livery stable, though. You might look there."

"Gracias," both of the men mumbled, and they took their leave.

"Why would Jorgé spend the night in the barn, with that pretty señorita waiting for him at the hotel?" Juan asked as he scratched the back of his neck.

Carlito, who had seen everything Juan had seen and

heard everything Juan had heard the night before, had come up with his own explanation. "Sometimes, Juan," he said, "you are too stupid to live."

"But I only asked—" Juan began.

"Silencio," Carlito hissed, cutting him off. "We go now to find the great Jorgé."

Down the empty street they walked, their boots scuffing up puffs of low dust. Juan said, "Why you call him 'the great' Jorgé, Carlito? Why you always call him that behind his back and not in front of his face?"

Carlito shook his head. "Do not make me shoot you so early in the morning, Juan."

"But Carlito . . . ?"

"It is *el sarcasmo*, Juan, the sarcasm. Do not ask me again."

They were nearly to the front of the livery before Juan said, "But what do you mean, 'sarcasm'?"

Carlito shot him a dirty look, that was all, but suddenly it was as if a lamp had suddenly been turned up in Juan's mind.

"Ah! It is like those times when you tell Señor Valdez that he looks very handsome today, or what a fine horseman he is, is it not?"

"Something like that." Carlito took hold of the rope handle on the livery door.

Juan was smiling. "I see. It is a polite lie, then, this sarcasm? When you say the opposite of what you mean in your heart?"

"Who's that!" came Jorgé's grumbling voice the moment Carlito swung open the cracked and creaking door. "Who's out there?"

"It is us, Carlito and Juan, Jorgé," Carlito announced. "Do not shoot."

"Wouldn't shoot you," came the answer as Carlito and Juan peered all around for the source of Jorgé's voice. Suddenly he stood up behind the boards of a stall. "I ought to knock the both of you silly for calling me from my sleep so early, though."

He tossed his blankets over the top rail of the half-height wall and stepped out into the main part of the barn, brushing straw from his arms and britches.

"Well?" he said, looking from Carlito to Juan and back again. "What you want?"

Juan shrugged. "It is morning," he said flatly, as if no other reason were needed.

"By your order, we have a fence to build," Carlito stated, putting the emphasis on *your order*.

"Why did you not sleep in the hotel last night?" asked Juan. "The señorita, she cries half the night. We heard her through the wall."

Jorgé's eyes narrowed. "You shouldn't have listened, Juan."

"We go now to the cantina," Carlito said before anything could actually get ugly. He was hungry and preferred to eat breakfast before there was any gunplay. "We will meet you there?"

"Yes, fine," Jorgé said, distracted by the blankets he was folding. "Just go."

Carlito and Juan muttered an overlapping *"Sí"* and stepped outside again.

Once outside with the door closed between themselves and Jorgé, Carlito grabbed Juan by his shirtfront and cruelly yanked him close. "You will not speak of the weeping señorita again. *Verdad?"* he breathed into the man's startled face.

Visibly shaken, Juan freed himself, moved off a few feet, and muttered, *"Santa vaca! Es verdad, Carlito.* No more señorita."

"Bueno," Carlito replied curtly as, with a puzzled Juan following in his wake, he headed back up the street toward Cantina Lopez and its promise of a good breakfast. Sooner or later.

• • •

"Fresh-squeezed juice of the orange, Slocum," Maria said, and he opened his eyes.

She sat beside him, smiling and holding a tray.

"Breakfast in bed?" he said. "What did I do to deserve this?"

She laughed a little. "You know very well, my big, handsome hombre. Come. Scootch up a little."

He moved back on the sheets until he was half sitting, and she placed the bed tray across his lap. It was a feast fit for a king! Eggs, probably five or six, scrambled with peppers and onions and cheese; a huge, fried ham steak, still sizzling; three thick slices of Texas-style toast with a pot of cactus jelly and another of extra butter; a big mug of coffee, and a tall glass of orange juice.

"My cousin, she sends me two crates every year. From California," she said proudly.

Hoping she meant the oranges, Slocum picked up the glass and took a long drink. He smacked his lips. "Say! That's good!" He took another drink. "This is livin' the life of luxury!"

Maria smiled and backed away. "I am bringing this to keep you distracted, you know. Come down when you are finished. Carlito and Juan, they are already here, and I expect Jorgé at any minute."

"Well, feed 'em a good, big breakfast, honey. I hope they're gonna need it."

She paused and turned, her hand on the door's latch. "If your wire comes in today, you mean."

"Yeah," he said, between bites of egg and ham. "Baby, you are one good cook and a half."

She winked at him and was gone.

He focused on the food, but he couldn't help wondering why the hell they were downstairs so early! The freight wagon wasn't supposed to pull in until eleven. He supposed he'd need to talk to the fellow at the livery, see about renting one of his buckboards to haul all that wire out to the place they'd left the posts.

He'd need to drop into the mercantile or the hardware, too, if Jaguar Hole had such a thing. They'd need tools with which to put up the wire, and seeing as how Valdez had supplied the muscle and the axes and saws, he thought that his side—meaning MacCorkendale—ought to supply the rest of the stuff they needed.

He sure wished MacCorkendale would send a man or two, though. It would be a help.

He ran out of orange juice before he was ready but managed to wash down the rest of his meal with coffee.

He really supposed he ought to have a little talk with Samantha, too, although he wasn't sure just how to fit it in. Just because she was loco, that didn't give him any call to be rude to her.

And rude was what he suspected she thought he was.

Breakfast finished, he took a long and satisfying piss out the rear window, then dressed for the day. He wondered just how it would go today with Juan and Carlito.

There shouldn't have been any "ito" on the end of Carlito's name. There was nothing diminutive about him, and he looked as if he didn't have to bother to butcher out a steer; he could probably just pick one up, on the hoof, and take a bite out of it.

And that Juan—he was a big boy, too, but he looked reasonably cowed by Carlito. And Jorgé. Jorgé cowed everybody.

Except him.

He strapped on his gun belt, checked his guns, slapped his hat on his head, then picked up the tray. Maria had carried it all the way up here. No reason for her to carry it down, too.

When he went downstairs, there sat his three cohorts, in the same chairs they'd occupied the evening before. Jorgé was the only one to greet him. "*Hola,* Slocum," he called with a wave of his hand.

Then Jorgé's eyes flicked to the tray, and he grinned wide. "You are the waiter now?"

Slocum grinned back as he slid the pillaged tray on the bar top. They were still the only customers in the place. It was only 6:45, after all.

"Just tryin' to get into shape for all that wire stretchin' we're gonna be doin'," he said.

He caught Maria's eye and added, "Mornin', darlin'. That orange juice sure hit the spot. Don't suppose I could have another glass?"

"Sí," she said, smiling. "I bring it to your table, Slocum." Chuckling softly, she motioned at him. "Go on, now. Shoo!"

She was beautiful. Simply beautiful.

He suddenly hoped the fence would take a very long time to build.

The freight wagon pulled in just before noon, and Slocum was waiting for it, along with Jorgé, Carlito, and Juan, and a buckboard he'd rented at the livery.

They loaded bale after bale of wire, the barbs sometimes puncturing their heavy gloves to leave bloody dots on their clothing and curses on their lips. Slocum had ordered what he thought they'd need to string a double row for ten or twelve miles, and it turned out to be more in person than what he'd pictured in his head when he'd ordered it.

The buckboard was piled high by the time they were finished.

They all sat down on the edge of the boardwalk in front of the freight station when they were loaded up, and assessed the damage to flesh and fabric.

Well, Slocum sat down to have a smoke as much as anything else.

Jorgé took off his gloves in disgust. "I forgot how much I hate the damned barbed wire. I have punctures in my puncture wounds."

"It'll be over soon, amigo," Slocum said as he put the smoke between his lips. He was punched full of little holes, too, and didn't like the wire any more than Jorgé did.

"I suppose it is a necessary evil," Jorgé said with a sigh.

Slocum nodded. "Yeah."

"Why?" said a new voice—Carlito. "I was hired to work the cattle, not hurt myself and them by sticking them with this stupid wire."

"You watch your tone, amigo," snapped Jorgé, and the way he said it made Slocum a little frightened, too.

However, Slocum recovered and said, "Carlito, nobody likes barbwire. But when two men own land that butts up together, and neither of 'em want to abide by the laws of free range, somethin's gotta be done. This is the only way Jorgé and I could see to do it without startin' another Mexican War."

Carlito scowled. "We call it the Gringo War."

"Suppose it all depends on which side you were on," said Slocum. "Like the War of Northern Aggression or the War to Free the Slaves."

"You have a point," Jorgé said, and stood up. "Let us gather our mounts and get on our way."

"I'm with you," Slocum said, and stood up, too. Anything to get away from talking to Carlito. He had enough problems without a cranky, fussbudget hand.

As he ambled over to the rail where Concho was tethered, he chanced a glance up at the hotel.

Furtively, Samantha peeked at him from behind her curtains.

Shit.

13

Pablo Valdez sat alone in his study, smoking his postdinner cigar and staring at the portrait of his wife, Salma. It hung opposite him, over the now-cold hearth, at the other end of the long room.

The portrait had been painted by one of Mexico City's finest artists, just before their marriage. Salma was not like he considered himself—a mongrel of Indian slaves and cold-hearted conquistadores—but half French and half Spanish, both lines pure. She was fair and copper-haired and had eyes the color of the sea—alternating between blue and green—and how beautiful she was!

Or had been. She was much younger than he, but their union had not produced any offspring. And she had grown fat. But still, he loved her.

He loved the sound of her voice, and the smell of her, and everything she said or thought or did.

Everything he did, he did for her.

Every move he made, he made with her future in mind. She was younger. She would be a widow someday, without his hand to guide her and see to her every need. Therefore, he had determined to be the best shepherd he could in this life.

He rolled his cigar ash into the crystal tray at his side. If they had made children together, perhaps things would have been different. It was not to be, though. Ten years of trying, ten years of praying, and nothing. He felt as if his loins were dust, unable to plant a seed.

It was not as if they hadn't tried. They had made love almost every night since their wedding day, in fact. Sometimes, more than once. In the beginning, much more.

Until lately. This business with MacCorkendale and his stubbornness over a few cattle made Valdez cranky and evil and out of sorts. Why could they not just each take the cattle on their lands and call it square? Cattle roamed. It was their nature.

But it was not the nature of men to exchange them over a country's boundary!

And now he had stooped to building a fence. Or letting his men put up one, anyway. Such foolishness. The first good windstorm would knock half of it down, he guessed. He had no plans to patrol it or keep it in repair.

And he was guessing MacCorkendale had no such plans, either.

Fingers tapped at his door.

"Come?" he said.

The door opened, and in stepped Salma, charming as always. And, as always, he stood while she entered. It was not just a male-to-female deference. She had been above him in social standing, and ten years had not erased that particular perceived gulf between them.

But Salma said, "Sit, my love. You will wear yourself out."

"If a decade of standing has not done it yet, my beloved . . ." he said, bowed slightly, and sat down. "However, as you will. Now, what can I do for you, *querida*?"

Salma bowed her head and looked up at him through her long, thick lashes, which were russet, the color of a red fox. "Could you spare me some time this afternoon, Pablito?"

He couldn't keep the grin from sprouting over his face. Pablito. It was her term of endearment for him.

"Of course, my dear Salma," he said. "What is it that you wish?"

She perched on the edge of his desk. "Could you try to forget about this dispute with Mr. MacCorkendale for an afternoon and come with me for a stroll in the gardens? They are at their most beautiful, and you have not set foot in them for months."

He didn't speak. He supposed that he had been overly occupied with MacCorkendale of late. And it was really such a petty thing, wasn't it?

"Pablito?"

He looked up at her and smiled. "Yes, my love. Forgive me. Of course I will go walking in the gardens with you. It would be my greatest pleasure. Thank you for reminding me."

"When you finish your cigar, then?"

"The very moment."

She leaned across the desk, then, and kissed him on the mouth rather chastely. He reached for her, but she pulled away, color flooding her cheeks. "For later, darling," she said, and left.

How strange, he thought, that God had granted him such passion with such a woman, only to bear no fruit. But such things were God's will, and not for a puny man, such as he, to fathom.

He returned to his cigar in an entirely new frame of mind.

Up at the MacCorkendales' ranch, Ralph MacCorkendale was having something of an epiphany.

As he stood out in the center of an empty paddock, staring out over the southern hills and grazing lands of his ranch, he came to a decision.

He had hired Slocum to go and shoot somebody—he didn't much care if it was Rodriguez or Valdez, himself—and by God, he wasn't getting his money's worth!

He was a penny-pinching man by nature as well as by upbringing, and he demanded value for his money. He wanted somebody dead and his cattle back, not some cockamamie fence!

"Bill!" he shouted. "Bill!"

A moment passed, and then Bill, a tough-looking, wiry sort of fellow and the best shot on the place, came around the side of the barn, a pitchfork in his hand. "Yeah, boss?"

"Saddle my horse. Your own, too. We're gonna take a little ride."

Bill nodded, then disappeared into the barn again.

"Bill?"

His grizzled head poked out again. "Yeah, boss?"

"Bring your guns."

Helga had been up on the porch, stewing and fretting, and accidentally overheard the conversation. It took a moment for its gravity to sink in, but when it did, she stood bolt upright and marched down into the yard and right over to where Ralph was waiting.

"No," she said, suddenly braver than she'd ever been, and not quite knowing why. "You will not make trouble with this fence. I forbid it."

MacCorkendale stared at her as if she were a rabid dog. Which she probably appeared to resemble. She imagined her eyes were wide and wild, at least.

At last he said, "What?"

It came out more as if he was stunned, rather than angry, and she was emboldened. She said, "You got no business out on dat desert, Ralph. If you want to send Slocum some help, you send a few of your men. But you are not going out there to start trouble."

He blinked rapidly. "Listen, this is my ranch. I'll do whatever I damn well please!"

"It is my ranch, too," she said and stood her ground. "When we signed the marriage papers, it became both of ours. You promised Papa. I hold you to it." She crossed her arms. "In fact, I say that my half is in the south. You got no business there unless I say so."

She suddenly realized what she was doing—the full impact of it, that was—and her face grew hot. She felt faint, but she tried to hold her ground, to stay upright.

Let him send her away! She would go with Slocum, and she would take half the ranch with her! Let him chew on that for a while.

But it seemed that MacCorkendale wasn't doing any chewing. He stared at her a moment before he said, "You called me Ralph."

She had? She didn't remember.

"Thank you, Helga. I don't believe you ever done that before." He looked practically staggered.

Helga knew she was, although for different reasons. She began to wobble and put all her concentration into staying upright and defiant.

MacCorkendale moved toward her, climbing the fence rather than using the gate in his hurry. He put hands on her shoulders, and said, "Helga, honey, are you all right? You don't look awful good."

Mustering her last bit of energy, she said, "No, I am not all right. Not if you are going to go down there and maybe get yourself shot. You leave that fence alone. It is the only chance we have to stop this foolish war you have with Mr. Valdez."

She wavered, but MacCorkendale's hands held her upright. For the moment. And then she felt herself crumpling to the ground, but not before MacCorkendale caught her and lifted her into his arms.

"Bill!" she heard him cry before the world went all the way dark. "Ride to town and get Doc Oaty!"

Slocum worked the posthole digger, taking turns with Jorgé whenever their backs gave out, and Carlito and Juan followed behind them, stringing and stretching wire.

They had begun the other way round, with Slocum and Jorgé doing the stretching, but Slocum grew tired of Carlito's complaints, and they soon traded. He and Jorgé were about three posts ahead of the wire gang, and they stopped for a moment.

"I bring up the wagon," Jorgé said. Slocum could tell this was harder on his friend than it was on him, and nodded. He didn't really want to trek back for just a new post, either. And his shoulder ached.

He plunked his butt on a boulder and pulled out his fixings bag. They'd fenced over two miles so far, by his reckoning, and he was ready to go back to town and rest his tired back and sore shoulder in a nice, soft bed. But he figured they'd best get another one or two in the ground first.

Tomorrow, they'd begin earlier. Maybe even stay out tomorrow night for an earlier start the next day.

About the same time that he touched fire to the end of his smoke, Jorgé drove the fence post wagon up alongside him.

"*¿Agua, amigo?*" Jorgé called.

"Be pleased."

Jorgé tossed him down the canteen, which he caught with one hand, then pried loose the cork. He took a long drink, then another. It was warm, but it was wet.

"You must have had great thirst, amigo," Jorgé said, smiling as he took the canteen and put it back up under the wagon seat. "You have emptied it."

"Sorry," Slocum said tiredly. "I'm about beat."

Jorgé sat down on the next boulder and ran his sleeve

over the back of his neck. "*Sí*, she is hot today, and I am not used to this kind of work."

"Who is?" Slocum said.

"True. And you have the wound in your shoulder. I am sorry, I forgot."

Slocum hadn't. The healing wound that had begun the day as a minor annoyance was now pounding to beat the band. "Ain't your fault, Jorgé."

The other man regarded his arm. "Slocum, I think she is beginning to bleed a little."

Slocum reached to touch the wound. His fingers came away red and damp. "Yeah," he said. "Well, it can't be helped."

"Yes, it can," Jorgé said, and stood up. "Come with me," he said, and led a curious Slocum back to the horses, which were tied to the back of the buckboard full of posts. He walked up to Concho. "Here," he said. "You go back into Jaguar Hole and let Maria tend to that. Maybe even see the doctor."

"Jorgé, I ain't leaving you boys out here to work on what was my idea in the first place!"

"And I will not have you bleed to death and therefore get out of it completely!"

Slocum began to chuckle, and Jorgé soon joined him. Slocum tightened Concho's girth, then stepped up on him. He hadn't realized until just then how sore his shoulder was, and he grunted a little with the effort.

"You see, amigo?" Jorgé said with a grin. "You go on. We follow quick enough."

14

Around nightfall, Bill came barreling into the ranch's yard and knocked on the front door. When MacCorkendale, having heard his arrival from upstairs, opened the door, Bill said, "Doc's comin' right behind me, boss. If you don't mind my askin', how's she doin'?"

"She's awake," MacCorkendale said. "Send Doc right in when he comes. Door's open." And then he turned his back and went upstairs again.

Behind him, he heard Bill say, "That's real good, boss. Just fine. I'll tell him."

MacCorkendale only grunted his acknowledgment.

He was suddenly too concerned about Helga to do more.

This afternoon, when she had shown signs of weakness, when she had fainted in the sun, he'd been shocked to his core. He'd always imagined Helga to be as strong as a draft mare. Anyway, that was how her father had represented her when he'd heard MacCorkendale was looking for a wife.

He'd sort of taken that description to heart and depended on her like a beast of burden: to do his laundry and cooking, to service his husbandly needs when he felt like it, to keep his house clean and his truck garden neat and weeded, and to never, never complain.

He hadn't really considered her human until today.

Of course, he supposed he'd loved her, in the way a man might love a good horse or a pet dog, but she was his wife, wasn't she? Didn't she deserve more than that?

And didn't he really feel more?

"Helga?" he called, halfway down the hall to his room. Her room, too. "Helga, are you all right?"

She waited until he poked his head through the door to answer. "I tell you, Ralph, I am fine. I don't know why I fainted. Will you let me get out of bed and go back to work? It's nearly suppertime!"

"No ma'am," he said in a voice that he hoped conveyed something like a benevolent command. "You'll stay right there. The doctor's on the way."

"The doctor?" Again, she blushed. See seemed to be doing a lot of that lately, didn't she. "Oh, Herr MacCorkendale, do not be silly. I am fine. Let me—"

"Herr MacCorkendale again? I like Ralph a whole lot better, Helga." He smiled, intending to comfort her.

But she seemed confused by the whole affair. Another reason he was glad the doctor was on his way.

He sat on the edge of the bed and took her hand in his. She had pretty skin, he realized. Now, why hadn't he noticed that before? A real pretty color, and soft, too. He stroked the back of her hand with his thumb.

"Ralph?"

"What, honey?"

"What is wrong?"

He smiled, for he heard the doc's buggy clattering into the yard. "Nothin's wrong, Helga. I'm just real glad you're still with us. You gave me quite a scare, you know!"

Her brow furrowed. "I am sorry. I did not intend—"

He heard the doc's footsteps on the stairs. "I know, Helga. Ain't your fault."

Knuckles rapped softly on the door. "Mind if I come in?" came Dr. Oaty's friendly voice.

MacCorkendale climbed to his feet, his wife's hand still in his. "Hell, no. Come on in, Doc. Been waitin' for you."

"Well, Bill was certainly in a state when he came up my porch steps," said the doctor. He was a stout man in his forties, with graying hair, a thick mustache, and a handshake that some said induced the need for medical attention.

However, MacCorkendale gave as good as he got, and the handshake ended in a draw. The doc moved to the far side of Helga's bed. "Now, why don't you tell me what happened, Mrs. MacCorkendale?"

Slocum, having ridden back to Jaguar Hole and put himself into Maria's hands, woke from a long snooze on her bed. It was dusk, and a bird was singing its last song until the morning. Soon, the owls would be out hunting their hapless prey.

He sat up, and the new tightness in his wound told him that Maria, after plying him with three whiskies, had stitched him up again—this time with horsehair, most likely.

Good. That wouldn't break.

He slipped on his clothes and made his way downstairs to the cantina. It was in full swing, and Jorgé and the others sat at a far table.

Jorgé spotted him, and shouted, *"¡Hola!"* across the noisy room.

Slocum waved a hand and sauntered over. "Evenin'," he said, and pulled out a chair.

"How is the shoulder, Slocum?" Jorgé asked.

"Better," Slocum admitted. "I think Maria sewed me up again."

"Bueno," said Jorgé. He signaled Diego, who came over directly. "Get my friend here some supper, and another round for me and the boys."

Diego looked at Slocum. "The usual, señor?"

"Yeah. Thanks, Diego."

Slocum watched as the little man navigated the crowd and made his way back into the kitchen, and then saw Maria peek out the window behind the bar and smile at him.

He smiled back warmly. Bless her heart!

She disappeared again, and he turned to Jorgé, saying, "Whatever happened to Samantha?"

Jorgé laughed. "Ah, it is all made up good, now, Slocum. She is mine, that girl. She waits for me at the hotel."

Slocum was dying to know just how that had happened, but he knew better than to push his luck. Instead, he said, "Well, what the hell are you doin' here, then?"

Jorgé grinned and shrugged. "It does her good to wait a little." And then he winked.

The formerly silent Juan seemed to get a kick out of this and started braying like a donkey. Carlito barked, "Shut up!" and that was the end of that.

Well, Carlito was just a barrel full of monkeys, wasn't he? Slocum thought.

He said, "You boys get much more of that wire strung after I left?"

"No," Carlito barked nastily.

"We got up to the last post you set," Jorgé said, and threw Carlito a dirty look.

Slocum had hoped for more, but he said, "That's fine, Jorgé, just fine."

Diego brought his supper and another round of drinks for the boys, and Slocum dedicated his full attention to his plate.

MacCorkendale had been sent from the room some time ago, and waited downstairs in the study, smoking a cigar and staring though the windows, out into the night.

Doc Oaty's tread in the upstairs hall got his attention, though, and he rushed out into the hall. "What is it, Doc?" he asked anxiously as the middle-aged man came toward him down the steps. "Is she gonna be all right?"

Doc stepped down to the landing, a smile on his face. "She is, MacCorkendale, if you let her take it a bit easy for the next few months."

MacCorkendale's face twisted up, and he said, "Huh?"

"You're gonna be a father, Ralph," the doctor said and slapped him on the shoulder. "'Bout seven months from now, give or take a week or two."

"Helga? She's. . . ." Words failed him. He said, "She's in foal?"

Doc Oaty laughed. "Well, I sure hope she isn't, although that'd tell us something about you, wouldn't it? But yes, she's in a family way. Congratulations."

In his excitement and confusion, Ralph said, "Cigar! You want a cigar, Doc? We've gotta celebrate my soon-to-be son!"

"Or daughter. And don't mind if I do, just so long as you offer again once the baby actually gets here!"

Ralph half ran to get him a cigar, and once he'd handed it over and shaken the doc's hand again, he suddenly remembered something. "Helga!" he announced, slapping his head.

"Yes, you should see to that," Doc said and bit the end off his smoke while Ralph raced up the stairs.

MacCorkendale didn't quite understand his excitement yet, didn't fathom why he'd been thinking about Helga in such flowery terms while he waited for Doc to come down. All he knew was that he had to see her, and right now.

He burst through the door, startling her.

"Helga!" he said, and realized he was weeping. He sat beside her on the bed and scooped her up into his arms. She resisted him at first, then relaxed into it. Oh, he'd crack that old-world reticence of hers eventually!

"Helga, darlin', we're gonna have a baby!"

She pushed back so that she could see his face. "You are not angry?"

"Angry? Why the hell should I be angry?" he roared, then got hold of himself. "Sorry, Helga. Didn't mean to shout. I'm not mad. Why, I'm so happy I about split a gut!"

She managed a tiny smile. "You did?"

"Hell, yes! Doc says it's comin' in about seven months or so. Try for a boy, honey, okay? Well, a girl'd be all right, I suppose . . ."

"I will try, Ralph."

"There," he said, almost tenderly. "You called me Ralph again."

"I suppose I did," she said with a tiny smile.

After a long walk in the sun-kissed garden, Pablo Valdez sat down for a leisurely meal with his beautiful wife, Salma. Servants brought in course after course, while Salma kept him pleasantly occupied with trivial conversation.

He did not take in much of what she actually said, preferring to let the sound of her lilting voice wash over him like some kind of angelic shower. Finally, halfway through the entrée, something she said sank in. "Preoccupied, darling?" she asked. "Is it that fence business?"

"No, my dear," he replied. "In fact, I had almost forgotten about it."

In truth, he had. The afternoon had been very pleasant and distracting.

"Good," she replied. "I am glad of it. I believe that this fence is a very good idea."

His brow furrowed. "You do, my dear? Why is that?"

"I lived in France for my first ten years," she said.

"I know."

"Well, in France, everything is fenced with wood or stone. Each man's livestock remains his. There is no wandering. Here, it is always MacCorkendale's cattle who cause the problem, or Antonio's or Esteban's. With fences, you will have no more problems. I cannot imagine why you did not think of this before."

Pablo simply stared at her. He couldn't think of a thing to say. Not that was fit for a woman to hear, anyway.

She picked up her fork. "I think it is very wise, this fence."

He couldn't stand it any longer. He shot to his feet, gripped the edge of the table, and shouted. "How little you know, my Salma!"

And with that, he simply thumped out of the room, marched to his den, and slammed the door behind him.

Slocum licked and nibbled at Maria's earlobe and felt the quiet little rumble of her giggle travel through his chest. "You like that, baby?" he whispered.

"I like whatever you wish to do," she said with a sigh. "You know that, my Slocum. Now, do it again."

He did, then worked his way down her long neck to her collarbone, then lower to the valley between her lush breasts. His hands he placed upon her breasts, cupping their fullness while he toyed with the nipples, already hardening and beading to pebbles as her excitement rose. He licked the sides of her breasts, then traveled lower, until he reached the flat of her belly and the tiny pelt of hair that covered her mounded delta.

He heard her sharp intake of air when he brushed the edge of that boundary with his tongue, then the flats of her palms on both sides of his head, urging him upward again.

"Take me now, Slocum," she breathed. "You are driving me wild."

He kissed her parted lips, and while he did, he entered her with tongue and cock simultaneously. She made a purring noise against his lips that vibrated his tongue and teeth and zigzagged down his spine.

As he began to move, her thighs slid up to hug his sides, only now growing slick with sweat, and she began to meet his every thrust and parry.

Faster and faster they moved, matching each other thrust for thrust, want for want, need for need. He felt her nails lightly rake his back, her teeth chew gently at his lip, then his shoulder.

And then, as they neared completion, her caresses became wilder, more intense. Her teeth raked his chest, his shoulders, and her moans became more urgent and fervid. He began to move harder into her, and faster, and not long after he did, she stiffened, back arched, neck craned back.

He pumped into her two, three times again and came with enormous force and fire.

They collapsed, still joined and panting in unison, in each other's arms.

"My Slocum," Maria managed to get out between puffs.

"Baby," he whispered and kissed her gently on the mouth. "Baby doll."

15

The next morning found Slocum and the men heading south again, toward their work. It also found him overhearing the conversation taking place behind him, between Juan and Carlito.

"Why you want to mess around with that whore?" Carlito was saying. "She only wants your money!"

"She is no whore," Juan said firmly. "Do not call her that again. And she can have all my money. I do not care. I love her."

There came the sound of Carlito spitting, then saying, "Love! What do you know about love? It does not exist!"

"I know more than you, Carlito," Juan retorted. "I know more than you ever will."

"You are a fool then, Juan," Carlito said and kicked his horse into a gallop, passing Slocum and Jorgé and moving rapidly ahead into the distance.

"Nice when the whole crew gets on so well," Slocum remarked around his quirley.

"It makes life the pleasure," Jorgé retorted with a straight face. "How many miles will we string today, Slocum?"

"Your guess is as good as mine," Slocum said. He was

hoping for three, at least, because he'd changed his mind about staying out here for the night. He didn't want to miss any chance to be with Maria, and that meant going back into town come nightfall.

Jorgé shrugged. "I think maybe we string three more. It is a good goal. We might even make four if we are lucky and the water holds out."

"True," Slocum muttered. His shoulder was feeling a good bit better today, but Jorgé had already decreed that posthole digging wasn't going to be on his work list today, so he had a hot day of stringing and stretching wire to look forward to.

Juan rode up next to them. "Did I hear right? We go back to town again in the evening?"

"Yeah," said Slocum. "That's the plan, anyhow."

Juan smiled. "Good. I am glad."

"You have got a girl, Juan?" Jorgé asked, then quickly added, "We couldn't help overhearing that little conversation you had with Carlito."

"Yes, I do," he said proudly. He leaned over in his saddle and said softly, "I think I will ask her to marry me. A good idea, no?"

"A fine idea!" crowed Jorgé.

"Congratulations," Slocum said, grinning. "Who's the lucky gal?"

"She is Conchita Elena Alba," Juan said. "You know her, Jorgé. The sister of Maria Anna Lopez."

Slocum started. "Maria's sister? If she looks anything like Maria, or even cooks anything like she does, you've got a catch, Juan."

Juan simply grinned from ear to ear.

Jorgé piped up, "You know about her little ones, Juan?"

"*Sí*, of course! They are my darlings!"

"What about Paolo Alba, Juan?" Jorgé asked, obviously playing devil's advocate. "What if he should return? What if he should want his wife again?"

"That is just it, Jorgé," Juan said happily. "He is not coming back. Not ever. Conchita, she got a letter from her cousin in Phoenix yesterday. Her cousin said that he saw Paolo shot dead in the street."

"And her cousin, he saw this himself?" Jorgé asked warily.

"He swears it by the Blessed Virgin."

Jorgé nodded. "Then it must be true. My best wishes for you, Juan."

Juan bowed his head quickly. "I thank you both. And I will work with Slocum today, with the wire. Carlito has the broader back for the fence posts. And today, the temper for digging the holes, I think."

"I cannot disagree with you on that account, Juan," Jorgé said with a laugh.

Slocum just grinned.

His mood still affable, Ralph MacCorkendale made ready to ride down to the south of his ranch, to help with the fencing. Somehow, it didn't matter so much anymore, this nonsense about open range. Of course he was still annoyed at Valdez for not being a good neighbor and returning his cattle, but what the hell. He had a son coming! Well, maybe a daughter. He could do what Helga wanted, just this once.

He took Bill with him, and Curly, too, figuring that six more hands would help that much more than his two, and they rode out of the yard at about ten in the morning. He took a last look up at his bedroom window.

Helga stood there, still in her nightclothes, and waved good-bye to him.

Christ, it was like he was seventeen again! Everything was good, everything made him feel cocky, everything gave him a rush of adrenaline!

He waved back, feeling pride swell his throat, and then cleared it. He said, "Race you to the halfway mark, boys!" and lashed his horse into a gallop.

Bill and Curly followed on his heels, but were careful to stay there.

They were well aware that you didn't beat the boss at anything, if you knew what was good for you.

Meanwhile, Pablo Valdez was leaving his rancho, as well. And in his company were also two men: Pepé, the luckless fellow who had ambushed Slocum and succeeded in winging him in the shoulder, and Ramon, a man who had been hired as much for his skills with a gun as those of a vaquero.

Valdez was still angry from the night before. He was angry that he had let his lovely wife distract him from more pressing matters, and also that he had actually listened to her for a moment, actually considered that this fence was a good thing! That *any* fence was good!

Well, she was half French, and therefore half crazy. He had known that when they wed. He liked it in some ways—especially in the bedroom—but not in others. In business, she was no good whatsoever.

And the same went for her feelings about this boundary they were constructing.

He had not even gone to bed last night but had stayed in his study and slept on the couch. He was afraid her nearness would make his heart soften.

Even, he thought, if it would make other parts of him hard as iron.

He smirked to himself, then straightened his face before looking toward his men.

"Let us ride, vaqueros!"

"Ye-ha!" screeched Ramon, and cut out ahead of them.

Pepé, having actually seen Slocum, was a bit more restrained. He said, *"Sí, patrón,"* and pushed his mount into a canter.

Fools, Valdez thought as he galloped along, quickly

catching and passing Pepé and gaining on Ramon. *I am surrounded by fools.*

Slocum and Jorgé had moved another mile down the fence by noon. Carlito was no easier to work with, but Juan was cheerful. All in all, Slocum thought, they were doing pretty well.

While they took a break in the shade of a lone cottonwood, passing the jerky and resting their tired bodies, Slocum said, "You think we can make another two miles before we call it a day, there, Jorgé?"

Jorgé finished chewing his jerky and swallowed before he said, "*Oh, sí, sí!* It is smooth land from here on. For a while, anyway."

They had been stretching wire up and down rocky slopes so far today, and this was good news to Slocum. Anything flat was good. And anything without rocks would likely be welcome news to the posthole diggers.

He wouldn't have sworn to it, but he thought he saw a glimmer of a smile cross Carlito's face at the mention of flatlands.

Having finished his share of the jerky, Slocum took a long drink of water, then got out his fixings pouch. He just about had the quirley rolled and ready when he heard hoofbeats approaching from the south.

Jorgé heard them, too, and stood up. "I wonder," he said, "has Valdez sent more help?"

The question was answered when Valdez, along with two hands, appeared on the top of the hill overlooking them.

Jorgé grinned and waved. "*¡Patrón!*" he called. "Welcome!"

Valdez didn't wave back. Neither did he shout an answer. He simply rode down the slope, his men behind him amid clouds of dust.

Slocum frowned and tossed his quirley aside. He rose, standing next to Jorgé. "I think we've got us some trouble," he said in a low voice.

Juan had scrambled to his feet, also, and looked a little frightened, but Carlito said quietly, "I hope you are right, Señor Slocum."

"Shut up, Carlito," snapped Jorgé.

Carlito bowed his head in a mock apology. "Pardon," he said sarcastically.

Valdez and his men rode down around the last wired post, giving a wide berth to the reels of wire set out on the ground, and up to the cluster of men under the cottonwood.

"Stop this," he said.

"Que?" asked Jorgé, and he appeared stunned.

"You have heard me. Stop this fencing. It is an abomination!"

Slocum said, "Now, hold on there, Señor Valdez. You yourself said it was the only thing to—"

"I do not care what I said!" Valdez broke in. He waved an arm in anger and spooked his horse in the process. He got it under control again and shouted, "This is what I am saying now!"

"Pablo . . ." Jorgé soothes, "can we not—"

"¡Silencio!" Valdez boomed, then gestured to the men with him. "Tear it down."

"A-all of it?" ventured Pepé.

"Every last post!"

"*Patrón*, what harm is there in letting what is there stand?" Jorgé asked in a calm voice. Slocum couldn't figure where that calm came from, but he sure as hell wasn't going to question it.

"These boys have worked awful hard," Slocum added.

"And Slocum, too, especially considering that he works with only the one good shoulder," added Jorgé, and threw a pointed glance at Pepé, who flushed and looked down.

"I do not care," Valdez snapped. "Carlito, Juan, get back to the rancho. You, too, Jorgé."

Jorgé frowned, and Slocum knew him well enough to know that when he frowned like that, everybody'd just better back off. Apparently nobody else caught this expression but Slocum, and he said, "Jorgé, just let it go."

But Jorgé wasn't paying any attention to him. Instead, he took a step toward Valdez's horse. "Then I quit, Señor Valdez," he said. "You are too stubborn and shortsighted a man to work for." Slocum saw his gun hand twitch and cringed a little. He knew how much damage that hand could do with a pistol in it.

Seemingly, so did Valdez, and this, if nothing else, brought the man back to reality.

"No, Jorgé," he said. "Do not quit. You have not yet been paid! And I have further plans for your services."

"*Sí,*" said Jorgé. "I am certain you do. And I am also certain that I would find these services very unpleasant to complete. Therefore, you have my resignation, señor."

Slocum knew just as well as Jorgé that Valdez was more than likely talking about his murder, and probably that of Ralph MacCorkendale, too. Why hadn't somebody drowned Valdez when he was a pup? It would have saved everybody a whole lot of trouble.

He said, "I'd accept it, if I was you, Valdez. If Jorgé said it, he means it."

Valdez said nothing but spat on the ground. Then he turned his horse around and headed around the end of the fence and up the hill. His two men went with him, and Juan and Carlito followed shortly. Juan appeared unhappy, probably because his chance to see Conchita again had just been bumped far into the future.

The poor SOB. Slocum vowed to tell Maria about it tonight. She could get word to her sister.

"Well," said Jorgé, sitting down once again, "there goes the match to my final bridge." He stretched his legs out before him. “Now Jorgé can do what Jorgé wishes.”

Slocum, still keeping his eyes on the crest of the hill Valdez and his men had disappeared over, said, “And what the hell does Jorgé wish? Want, I mean.”

Jorgé pulled his sombrero down over his eyes. “To take a siesta, Slocum. Just a siesta.”

16

Five minutes later, MacCorkendale and his boys came loping up, and Slocum kicked Jorgé's boot until he woke up. They were both on their feet by the time MacCorkendale stepped down off his horse and asked, "What's goin' on? I thought Valdez loaned you a couple of men."

"He unloaned 'em," Slocum said.

"When?"

"Five, maybe ten minutes ago," replied Jorgé, then yawned.

MacCorkendale muttered, "Well, that son of a bitch!" and then, in a normal tone, added, "We're here to help you boys now. This here's Curly and Bill."

"I'm Bill," said the wiry one.

"And I'm Curly," the broader one said.

Slocum stuck out his hand. "Pleased to meet you both. We were just takin' a break."

"Take your time," MacCorkendale said. "Us three'll get started. You got wire pullers?"

Slocum handed his over. "Posthole digger's over there," he said with a wave of his hand.

"Fair enough," MacCorkendale said. He and his boys turned and went to work.

"Nice," said Slocum, with no small degree of satisfaction.

"Bueno," agreed Jorgé, and settled in again, pulling his hat low.

Slocum sat down and got out his rolling pouch again while he watched MacCorkendale, Bill, and Curly go to work. It was turning out to be a real peculiar day.

How could she be pregnant?

Helga told the doctor it had been at least six weeks since MacCorkendale had made love to her, but he said that did not matter. Of course, Helga's menses had never been normal—according to her mother—but still, it seemed that she should have known.

Dr. Oaty's examination had been thorough, though—embarrassingly so—and he was a real doctor. He would know these things.

Still, she had her secret doubts. Why was she not nauseous in the morning? Why was she not craving many odd foods?

She was having a very smooth pregnancy, Dr. Oaty had said. And when he had asked if she was finding that her skirts fit a bit tight lately, she'd had to admit that yes, they did.

But that could be explained, couldn't it? Perhaps she had been eating a little more than usual. She had taken a second helping of this or that more often recently.

Especially desserts. Especially when she made *Apfel Kuchen.*

She stared at her hands, still soft despite the years of scrubbing floors and washing dishes. Would they still be soft enough to touch her baby and not hear it cry at the chafing?

And MacCorkendale. He was happy now, proud as a cock, but how would he be in years, when the newness had gone away, and he was left with the same old wife and a sullen boy or self-absorbed girl child?

Helga raised her hands and cupped her face in her palms. She began to weep.

Pablo Valdez held up a hand, calling a halt to his men's leisurely jog home.

"*Patrón?*" Carlito inquired. "What is it?"

Valdez turned his horse around to face them.

"Carlito, Juan, you know these men. You have worked shoulder to shoulder with them. Do *you* think they have gone away? That they have stopped the fencing?"

Juan kept his peace, but Carlito said, "*No, patrón.* I do not think so. Slocum is very stubborn, almost as stubborn as Jorgé."

"You think they would continue, even without your help, even when MacCorkendale has sent no one, not a single vaquero, to help them?"

"*Sí*, I do," Carlito said. Although Valdez noticed that he left himself a way out with an added, "Of course, it is only my opinion," and a little bow of his head.

"Your opinion is what I asked for, Carlito."

A mean smile bloomed on Carlito's face.

Valdez did not much care for Carlito, but the man was good at what he did. And the unspoken employer-employee contract did not have a friendship clause, he reminded himself.

"Turn around, vaqueros," he said. "We are going back. We will see just what is happening."

"And if they are still building, *patrón*?" Carlito asked.

"We will cross that bridge when we come to it," Valdez muttered. He sincerely hoped they wouldn't have to. "Keep to a slow jog, men. We will not want to announce ourselves with billowing dust."

Slocum looked up from the wire he was pulling. Hoofbeats?

Muffled and far off, but they certainly sounded like

hoofbeats, nearing them from the south. He squinted, looking for a dust cloud such as the one he seen just before Valdez and his men showed up, but there was none.

He noted that Jorgé had stopped in his labors, too, and had turned his attention southward. Without looking over at Slocum, he said, "A few cattle, you think?"

"Hope so." They both knew what it meant if Valdez had returned.

MacCorkendale, Bill, and Curly were far out ahead, digging holes and setting posts. They hadn't heard anything. Slocum gave out a low whistle, and MacCorkendale thankfully turned his head. Slocum signaled him, and quickly, MacCorkendale got his men back behind the post wagon, which they'd only just pulled up beside them.

"C'mon, Jorgé," he whispered, and the two of them slipped around behind the wire's buckboard.

They waited.

And waited.

And waited.

No sound came to Slocum's ears. He was beginning to think he was sunstroked, that was all, and hearing things, when he saw movement along the ridge at the top of the hill.

Jorgé started to move out of the wagon's cover, but Slocum grabbed his arm and nodded toward the crest.

"What?" said Jorgé.

"Shh!" Slocum hissed, and whispered, "Left of center. Blue."

Carlito had been wearing a blue checkered shirt when he rode out.

In a moment, Jorgé whispered, "I see him. The bastard."

The mare that one of MacCorkendale's men had been riding suddenly whinnied. Her call was answered by a poignant neigh from the other side of the hill.

"So much for cattle," Jorgé said with a shrug.

"Yeah," replied Slocum, just as a shot rang out and chipped the wood a half foot from his head.

"Jesus!" he snarled. "That was too close!"

Jorgé was already firing toward the hilltop.

Not Slocum, though. He figured he'd have a lot better chance of hitting something—and boy, did he want to hit that Carlito!—if he had a long gun, and he made his way toward the end of the wagon, where Concho was tethered.

"Swing right!" he commanded, and when the horse started to swing left, he said, "No swing right you idiot!"

Concho immediately corrected himself and swung his butt clear back around the backside of the wagon.

"Good boy, good fella," Slocum said, and crouching, crept forward and slid his rifle from its boot. "Stay put and keep your head down, if you know what's good for you," he added before he scurried back to Jorgé.

"Thank you for bringing mine, too," Jorgé said sarcastically.

"Couldn't get to it," Slocum said, and took aim at that tiny patch of blue on the hill. He fired, and heard a yelp.

"Atta boy!" MacCorkendale cried joyously.

He was a little premature, if you asked Slocum.

He kept on shooting but couldn't tell what he was firing at. Apparently, those other boys had owned the sense to find better natural blinds than Carlito.

Still, he was worried about how many rounds MacCorkendale and the others were firing toward the hill. He hollered to get MacCorkendale's attention, then motioned for him to slow the shooting down. He held up a cartridge, and MacCorkendale took his meaning.

The fire from the post wagon slowed down to just enough to keep the men on the hill shooting at them, when Jorgé brushed by him. "I get the damn thing my own self," Jorgé whispered and was gone.

Slocum, stuck with the job of covering him, fired rapidly toward the hilltop, the thing he had just cautioned MacCorkendale against.

Jorgé disappeared around the far side of Concho. Slocum flicked his eyes away from the hill just in time to see Jorgé's arm dart over Zorro's saddle and snatch his rifle from its boot. He was just coming around Concho's head again when he went down.

"*¡Mierda!*" he cried, then, "*¡Santa Maria!*"

"Aw, shit," Slocum muttered, and ran toward him. He grabbed Jorgé's wrist with one hand and Jorgé's rifle with the other, and quickly dragged him back behind the wagon.

"That was real smart," Slocum growled as he checked the man over.

"Thank you," replied Jorgé with a wince. "It is my leg, you fool, not my arm!"

"You're not just whistlin' Dixie." Slocum had eased back Jorgé's bullet-torn pant leg to reveal a bloody mess, most of which had trickled into his boot. The bone stuck out from his shin like a jagged tree limb. "Bad news, amigo. She's busted, for certain sure."

"This is getting us nowhere!" Valdez said and tossed rocks at his men to get their attention.

"But I have just shot Jorgé!" Ramon complained. "He is down!"

"Don't raise your voice to me," Valdez snapped, and gestured. "Go wide. And do not shoot until you can actually see them. *¿Es verdad?*"

As one, the men nodded and split into two groups, each one taking a different side of the hill—Juan and Carlito, his arm bound up in a makeshift sling, worked their way west, toward where Slocum and the wounded Jorgé were hiding, and Pepé and Ramon went to the east, toward MacCorkendale and his two men.

A nasty smile curled Valdez's lips. "We will see now," he muttered, "we will just see who is in charge of this range!"

Clutching his gun, he hurried after Pepé and Ramon.

17

Maria pushed open the front door of the casita with her hip, mainly because her hands were full. She carried a platter of tamales, beans, and tacos to her mother and sister and niece and nephew each afternoon in this manner. God forbid that for once, Mama or Conchita could come and get it themselves.

"Mama?" she called.

No answer.

She walked through the small main room to the kitchen area and placed her burden down on the table. Where could they all be? They had known she was coming.

Her face wrinkled into a scowl. She went out the back door and called down the alley. "Mama? Conchita?"

Nothing.

"Consuela! Alberto!"

And then she heard a rustle from behind her, at the house's front door. She turned round to see them squeezing through the front door, all at once, like a flock of sheep through a half-open gate.

"Maria!" cried Mama, clapping her chubby hands together. "How fortunate that you have come!"

"I always come, Mama," Maria said, puzzled. "I brought you lunch."

"What you bring today?" asked Alberto, his dark, little boy's eyes full of mischief. "Tacos, *Tía* Maria? I love tacos!"

"Yes," she said as he raced past her to the kitchen. "And more. Mama, what is going on?"

Conchita—who, for once, was not drunk—said, "Oh, Maria! It is so wonderful!" and she twirled, a load of parcels in her arms.

It was, indeed, past wonderful to see Conchita sober and happy, and Maria wondered how long this had been going on. Despite the fact that they lived only a hundred yards distant, she had not seen her sister for at least three weeks. She was normally passed out in the back room when Maria made her visits. Perhaps, for the last few, she had not been there at all!

"What is so wonderful?" Maria asked.

Mama said, "Conchita is to be married again," and smiled broadly. "She has found a beau."

It was a good thing Maria was standing beside the sofa, because it broke her fall, and she landed sitting up, although somewhat haphazardly. "A beau?" she stammered. "How? When?"

"Look at the material for my wedding dress, and I shall tell you," Conchita bubbled.

"I do not like this, Carlito," Juan said as they stealthily circumscribed the largest clumps of brush on their way across the back of the hill.

"We have worked beside Slocum and Jorgé," he continued. "We are amigos."

Carlito, who was leading the way, stopped and turned, keeping low. "Maybe your amigos, Juan. Not mine. This fence, she is a big mistake from the beginning. I have known it all along."

"Then it is true? You only work on the fence because Señor Valdez, he says to?"

Carlito started moving again. *"Sí."*

Juan came to a dead stop. "Then I am no better than you if I do this," he said, disgusted. He found a rock and sat on it. "I quit, too, just like Jorgé."

Carlito whirled around, and it startled Juan so much that he nearly fell off his rock.

Carlito said, "You cannot quit. It is too late. Señor Valdez, he expects you to go down there. And Señor Valdez is a man who it is not wise to disappoint."

Carlito's tone implied that Juan had better not disappoint him, either.

But Juan held his ground. And in addition, he leveled his pistol. "I am quitting."

Carlito backed off from the gun, but his expression didn't change. "There is always later, Juan. I will come for you."

"Only if Señor Valdez tells you to," Juan said. "I am not much worried. Slocum—he or Jorgé—will kill you anyway."

Carlito turned away without a word—but with a filthy glare—and continued creeping.

Slocum, having quickly ripped open Jorgé's pant leg and applied a tourniquet, turned his attention to other matters. The fact that Valdez's men had stopped firing, for one.

Jorgé's wound was serious, but he'd done all he could do for now. At least there was a doctor in town, although Slocum doubted that Jorgé would much appreciate the ride back.

He figured that Valdez had either given up and gone home—highly unlikely—or split his forces and sent them to opposite sides of the hill. That was the option he was putting his money on.

To Jorgé, who was still flat on the ground, he said, "Can you cover me if I go out there?"

"Help me scoot under the wagon, and I can," came the reply.

Slocum got hold of his good leg and gave him a shove. Jorgé yelped, and Slocum said, "That's right. Stir up some sympathy."

"Screw you," came the reply as Slocum rounded the far end of the wagon.

Keeping low, he scuttled to the fence, under it, then to the base of the hill and along that base. When he heard a scuffing sound, he stopped dead and listened hard.

There it was again. Someone was making their way toward his old position, about thirty feet up the hill from where he presently stood.

He moved over a couple of feet, taking cover behind a scraggly sage, then held very still, alert for the slightest sound.

And then someone shouted, "Jorgé! Carlito's coming your way!"

Suddenly, Carlito stood up from nowhere—Slocum thought he must be part Apache!—and wheeled to fire behind him. Before he could, though, Slocum's slug put him down. Carlito tumbled down the hill and few yards, then lay still, shot through the neck.

From under the wagon, Jorgé shouted, "*¡Gracias, Juan!*"

"*De nada,*" came the lackadaisical reply.

Slocum could practically see Juan shrugging, and choked back a chuckle. There were other men out there, stalking them.

Quickly considering his options, he decided to go around the hill and come up behind them. Hopefully. Maybe, if Juan was in the right mood, he could pick him up on the way. Two guns were always better than one.

But he was still a little suspicious of Juan, and so moved forward and upward in a crouch, and carefully. He spied Juan about ten minutes later, perched on a lone boulder and smoking a black cigarette.

He aimed his Colt, low.

"Juan!" he hissed.

Juan went for his gun automatically, but stopped short when he saw it was Slocum. He waved lazily. *"Hola, amigo,"* he said.

Slocum cast a glance over the hillside but couldn't see anyone else. "It safe?" he whispered.

"Sí," Juan replied. Then he added, "If you have taken care of Carlito."

Slocum holstered his weapon and stood up. It felt good. "I have. You in the mood to team up with me?"

Juan shrugged. "I have quit my job. I am looking for a new one."

Now, Slocum knew that Valdez and the rest of his men had a lot longer hike to make than he had just accomplished, but still, time was of the essence. He said, "You're hired."

"By whom?"

"By me, until I tell you different."

Juan cocked his head. "And what are you paying?"

Christ! thought Slocum, but he said, "I'll pay for your wedding, all right?"

Juan hesitated a moment, shrugged, then nodded his head. "A deal."

Pablo Valdez and his men had heard the shot that killed Carlito, and he'd motioned them down in the dirt. When it was followed by nothing but silence, though, he motioned them slowly up again.

He knew someone had been killed. There would have been more shots if not.

But who? There was no time to go and check. He would just have to hope that the death had occurred on MacCork-endale's side, and go on.

Softly, he said, "Onward, men."

Pepé and Ramon started forward once again, in a low crouch.

When he noticed Pepé hanging back a little, Valdez picked up a rock and chucked it at him.

The rock found its mark in the back of Pepé's head, knocking his hat awry, and Pepé grumbled "Ow!" as he looked back, then silently moved ahead.

Slocum and Juan silently followed in Valdez's footsteps.

And then, at last, just before Valdez and his men rounded the hill, Slocum caught sight of Valdez's sombrero. He motioned Juan down, then said, "Hold up there, Valdez."

He'd expected Valdez to whirl around in surprise, but he didn't expect him to whirl, firing.

Which he did.

Slocum hit the dirt as a slug whizzed past his ear, cursing himself for not waiting until he was closer, or not waiting until he had all three men in sight. He imagined Juan was just plain cursing him.

Valdez, on the other hand, was cursing him out loud.

"Where are you, you son of a bitch?" he shouted, paying no heed to MacCorkendale or the men he had with him. Slocum prayed they'd have the presence of mind to move on up the hill, and thus catch Valdez's men in their crossfire.

But he couldn't count on it.

Aiming his rifle up through the scrub toward the sound of Valdez's voice, he got off three quick shots, then waited. He heard a distant thump, and then all hell broke loose.

Slugs cut brittle branches all around him, dug into the hard clay soil, but miraculously, he was untouched by the time it stopped.

"Slocum?" It was MacCorkendale's voice. "Slocum! You all right?"

"Breathin'," called Slocum.

He slowly got to his feet, to see MacCorkendale and his men slowly poking around in the brush. Valdez was the only surviving member of his party, although he was shot in the upper arm and none too happy about it.

He glanced behind him. Juan was still facedown in the dirt somewhere. He called, "MacCorkendale, Juan is with us now. Tell your boys not to shoot!"

Juan slowly rose from the brush, only to receive a verbal lashing from Valdez, who was leaned up against a rock and spewing Spanish invectives like a proverbial fishwife. Juan said, "Shut up, old man. I do not work for you anymore."

"Where's the other one?" MacCorkendale asked.

"Taking the bath of dirt," Juan said.

Slocum poked a thumb in the direction from which they'd come. "Other side of the hill. Hey, Juan? Go get Valdez's horse, would you?"

"You buy the wedding cake, too?"

Slocum rolled his eyes and said, "Yeah, the goddamn cake, too. Just get the horse, will you?"

Slocum spoke at length to Valdez, explaining that guards would be posted lest Valdez send back more armed men. He was also informed that he could send two men—unarmed—to retrieve the bodies, and, in no uncertain terms, that since the wire was being strung on the American side of the border, it was none of his damned business.

Of the latter, Slocum wasn't entirely sure. In fact the whole positioning of it had been a guess on everybody's part. The actual border might be two or three feet—or miles—either way, he figured. But for now, it didn't matter.

He emptied Valdez's guns, got him up on his horse, and sent him on his way.

"Should'a killed him," MacCorkendale muttered. "Gonna make more trouble."

"But not today," Slocum said gruffly.

He left MacCorkendale, Juan, and Bill to work on the fence and Curly on guard while he unloaded the rest of the wire so that he could haul Jorgé back to town in the buckboard.

"Sorry to make you so much bother, amigo," Jorgé said.

"Don't speak so soon," Slocum said as he sucked at yet another barb-punctured finger. "I ain't loaded you in the wagon, yet."

Jorgé's brows furrowed. "*Sí.* That will smart quite a bit, I think."

Slocum split one of the fence posts into thinner strips and made a crude splint for Jorgé's leg. Then he, with MacCorkendale's help, loaded Jorgé into the wagon bed. This was naturally accompanied by a great many curses from Jorgé.

"Ride back's gonna be fun," Slocum muttered.

MacCorkendale said, "Hit a rut for me."

From the back of the wagon came, "I am hearing you, you friends! *¡Mierde!*"

Slocum climbed up into the wagon's seat, tipped his hat to MacCorkendale, and set out for town.

Halfway there, he slugged Jorgé into insensibility, just to keep the noise level down to a dull roar.

18

Later that night, while a newly casted and sedated Jorgé was at the hotel under Samantha's care—Slocum had only had a moment to speak to her privately but found that he hadn't needed to, for she had figured the situation out for herself and had now resigned herself to stick with Jorgé—Slocum lay in bed with Maria snuggled under his arm.

They had made love twice already, and most satisfactorily, and Slocum was enjoying a decent cigar and a bottle of champagne that Maria had surprised him with. Sweat glistened on their nude bodies, and Slocum had balanced his ashtray on her belly.

The night air was still, and he blew smoke rings, through which Maria lazily poked her fingers as she tried to collect them, with little success. He whispered, "How big a wedding does your sister expect to have?"

Maria's brow furrowed prettily. "And how do you know that my sister plans to marry? I just learned this myself this afternoon!"

He grinned. "Juan told me."

"But why do you want to know how big her wedding will be?"

He hugged her shoulders. "It's a long story, honey, but it looks like I'm payin' for it."

Juan had taken off for town once the workday was done, but MacCorkendale could hardly wait to get back to the ranch and his unborn heir. Well, Helga, too. Valdez had sent a couple men—unarmed—to pick up the bodies, and they'd left, with no further incidents.

Today, at least.

MacCorkendale was tired. They'd strung at least another mile of wire, and it was the sort of work that he wasn't at all accustomed to. But Juan had been reasonably good natured about explaining what had to be done—and in what order—and they had proceeded.

Now he lay in bed, in the dark, beside Helga, the future mother of his child.

He felt something new, something grand and special for her. Something that he had expected to feel all along, but had not, at least, not until today. There was suddenly a tender place in his heart, a place that only Helga could fill.

"Helga?" he whispered. "Helga, my love?"

She stirred slightly, and he repeated, "Helga?"

"What is it?" she asked sleepily. "What is wrong?"

"Nothin', honey," he said as he felt his erection growing. "Just wondered if you were awake, that was all."

Daintily, she yawned. "I am now. What time is it, Ralph?"

"Don't know. Helga, when the doc was here, he didn't say nothin' about . . . about you makin' love, did he?"

The question seemed to surprise her, and she hesitated a bit before she said, "He did not."

"I mean, he didn't say as how it would hurt the baby?"

"Nein."

He rolled toward her and put his hand on her cheek. The moonlight from the window bathed her face in pale light, and he wondered how in the world he had been wed to her for two years and never noticed what beautiful skin she had, what lovely coloring, and what lovely, light eyes.

"Helga, would you, that is . . . would you mind . . . ?"

She seemed to soften toward him. Something passed over her eyes—he couldn't decipher it—but then she whispered, "I would like to, Ralph. It has been many weeks."

She let him take her nightgown all the way off—something she had never done before—and she lay there beside him, all naked and ripe and voluptuous, like the model in a painting. He trailed the tips of his fingers over one full, creamy-skinned breast, then the other, and he heard her little intake of air, almost a gasp.

He let his hand drift lower, then lower as he watched her eyes grow round.

"R-ralph, what are you doing?" she stammered.

"Just tryin' to make it . . . nice. For you, too, I mean." He dipped his fingers between her legs and found her moist and slippery, wetter than she'd ever been for him.

His erection was about to explode, and so he eased himself over her, parting her thighs with his knees. "You're sure I won't hurt the baby?" he asked as he positioned himself.

"Yes, I am sure," she said and smiled at him. The smile of a madonna.

He entered her as if for the first time.

Pablo Valdez sat, shirtless, on the edge of his bed while Salma fussed with his bandages. He hadn't needed a doctor. He'd been lucky, she'd said, lucky that the bullet had passed cleanly through him, without so much as chipping a bone.

In the old days, he supposed they might have run a hot poker through the wound to cauterize it and keep it from rotting him from the inside out, but Salma had ointments she applied that could heal like magic. She had brought them with her when they came from Mexico City, and her mother had brought them before, when the family came to the New World from France.

His shoulder still hurt like the devil, however, and she had made him some tea to help with the pain. It tasted as bitter as death itself, although he was too polite to admit it, but he had to confess that it was easing his pain somewhat.

Thank goodness for Salma.

But damn that Slocum, and especially Jorgé! His men were deserting him like rats climbing down the ropes of a sinking ship! If he ever saw that Juan again . . .

Salma finished and stood up, taking his soiled bandages with her. She touched his face and said, "You will live, my darling. Did the tea help?"

"Yes, Salma, it seems to. Thank you."

"Pablo?"

"Yes?"

"You must divorce yourself from this anger you are feeling. Times change. We must change with them."

As always, her words made sense. And, as always, he did not want to hear them.

"Salma?" he said. "Send for Miguel Cordura. He would be at the bunkhouse."

Her eyes narrowed. "Why?"

"Do not trouble yourself. Just send for him. I wish to speak with him."

Salma nodded and departed. And ten minutes later there was a knock on his door.

"Come," said Valdez.

In walked Miguel Cordura, who had been with Valdez since the beginning. Miguel was a seasoned man, a fast and accurate man with a gun—or at least, he once was—and a man he could trust.

Not like Juan or Jorgé.

"¿Patrón?" Cordura said, sweeping off his hat and bowing.

Respect, thought Valdez. *There is nothing like a little old-fashioned respect.*

"Miguel, you are still a good man with a pistol, no?"

Cordura stood a little taller and smiled, just slightly. "Yes."

"And you are not opposed to using it for your employer?"

Miguel's smile widened. "Just what did you have in mind, *patrón*? You know I will do whatever you bid."

Slocum awakened still entangled in Maria's arms. When they had finished their lovemaking the night before, they had been too tired to move another inch and had fallen asleep with Maria's legs still wrapping his back, his arms still hugging her tightly, and his head cradled upon her breast.

He tried to disentangle himself without waking her, but found it about as easy as uncoiling a sleeping snake.

Her eyes fluttered open, and she smiled. "Good morning, my Slocum," she whispered huskily.

He slumped down into the position he'd woken in. "Mornin' yourself, baby." He brushed a kiss over her temple.

She trailed her fingertips across his jaw. "And how is your shoulder this morning? There is a chance you would take a day off from your labors to rest it?"

He smiled. "Sorry, honey. Its healin' up fine. No excuses for me."

She sighed. "It was worth a try."

"You know what I could use?"

"Don't tell me. Breakfast?"

"Right again, Maria," he said with a grin, and rolled off of her.

She sat up, gathering the sheet to her. "You men," she said, shaking her head. "If it is not the sex, it is the food."

"Shameless, ain't we?" he said, grinning.

She laughed, stood up, and walked about the room, gathering her clothing. "*¿Huevos?*" she asked. "With some nice smoked bacon, and maybe those potatoes, the way you like them?"

"Home fries. Yes'm. That'd be great." He pulled on his britches, then sat down to tug on his boots.

"And you have everything settled with the señorita? The one across the way?"

He started a bit. He thought she'd forgotten all about Samantha. But he said, "The misunderstandin's all took care of, honey."

"I thought so," she said, nodding. "I just wanted to hear it from your lips."

He stood up and walked around the bed. "And I only want to kiss yours, baby." He kissed her deeply, running his hands up underneath the blouse she'd just put on, cupping her breasts, running the flat of his thumbs over her nipples.

She giggled, then pushed away. "You had better watch yourself, Señor Slocum, or there will be no food fixed and no fencing for the whole of this day."

"Okay, okay," he said, grinning. "Consider my wrists slapped."

She backed up a step and tucked in her blouse. "And Slocum?"

"Yes?"

"Be careful when you piss out the window, my darling. Yesterday you hit my second cousin's mule. He was not amused."

"Your cousin or the mule?"

She opened the door. "Neither one."

By the time Slocum got downstairs, Jorgé was waiting for him, his crutch leaned against the wall, with Samantha in tow.

He noticed that she made certain to sit as close to Jorgé as possible and didn't speak to Slocum unless it was absolutely necessary.

She was, perhaps, smarter than he had given her credit for.

Juan joined them just as Diego came to take their order, and he was in fine fettle, indeed.

"I tell Conchita you are paying for our wedding," he said happily. "She is very glad, very grateful."

Slocum didn't ask just who she was grateful to. The smile plastered onto Juan's face told the whole story.

"You pay for their wedding, Slocum?" Jorgé asked.

Slocum explained, briefly.

"Hell," said Jorgé. "Juan, I would have thought better of you. But if Slocum's paying, I will pay, too. You saved my bacon as much as his."

Slocum arched a brow at this unexpected bit of generosity but didn't say anything to get Jorgé to change his mind. It was fine with him if Jorgé wanted to split the bill.

Diego came out from the kitchen soon enough and set a steaming, fragrant plate before each of them, along with a pot of coffee. There was also a tall glass of orange juice, just for Slocum.

"Why does he get orange juice and we don't?" he overheard Samantha ask Jorgé in a whisper.

"He sleeps with the squeezer," was Jorgé's reply.

Slocum smiled and dug into his eggs.

19

Jorgé had hobbled off to the hotel—his crutch under one arm and Samantha under the other—and Slocum and Juan had departed the cantina for their fence a good half hour before a worried Diego came into the cantina's kitchen.

"Maria?" he asked in an odd tone.

She crooked a brow. "What is it?"

"There is a man."

"There are many men, Diego, and they all want tequila or cerveza or breakfast or all three." She slid another pan of enchiladas into the oven. "What is so different about this one?"

"He asks for Slocum. And Jorgé. And Juan. And he looks like he is up to no good."

She wiped her hands on her apron and scowled. "Is he Mexican or American?"

"Mexican, Maria. His name is Miguel Cordura."

"What did you tell this Señor Cordura?"

"I say that I do not know. I say that I will ask you."

She nodded. "You did right, Diego. Is he out front now?"

"Yes, at the corner table." Diego slanted his glance out the little window behind the bar. "He watches us, so no slipping out the back door." He winked at her.

Damn! That had been her first thought, to waylay Cordura as long as possible, but if he was watching her . . .

"Tell him that I am very busy, Diego," she said. "But that I will come and speak with him as soon as I have the time."

She immediately picked up the plate of flour tortillas she had just finished making and began to fill them and put them into a baking pan. As Diego left, she called—just loud enough that it would be heard throughout the cantina—"Tell him I am a busy woman with much work to do, Diego. My time, she is at a premium!"

From the corner of her eye she watched the man scowl. Too bad. He would have to wait. She didn't like the looks of him, anyway. He was ugly, mean-looking and hard-faced, as if in his day he had killed many a man and not cared a bit about any of them.

She did not look forward to speaking with him, but she would have to.

And she would have to lie to him. Would he know?

Probably.

That kind usually did.

When Ralph MacCorkendale left for work the next day—taking along Bill and Curly—he left behind, for the first time, a tearful Helga. Not that she hadn't cried when he'd left before, but that had been in relief or frustration. Or both. This time, it was that she hated to see him leave her sight.

He had been wonderful last night. So tender, yet masterful, and for the very first time, he had made her feel that incredible, special pleasure that before, she could only bring to herself in secret.

For the first time, she had felt as if she were truly loved.

She wiped away her tears with a corner of her apron. If only it could go on like this forever!

Her hand dropped to her stomach, and she let it linger

there, thoughtfully. How soon, she wondered, would she feel the life stirring within her? She willed it to move, to do something that would prove to her that it was there. But there was nothing, no tangible sign of life.

"In time," she whispered to herself. "It will come in time."

Ralph and his tiny dust cloud had disappeared over the horizon by the time she closed the screen and went back into the house. She had decided to make him something special for his dinner. One of his favorites. Chicken-fried steak with mashed potatoes and gravy, she thought.

She smiled and, humming, made her way up the stairs to take a little nap. She was tired already.

Slocum and Juan reached the fence line only moments before MacCorkendale and his men. Slocum had brought back the buckboard, and they spent the first ten minutes reloading the baled wire.

Once again, he sent Curly up on top of the hill to watch for any danger from the south. He wouldn't put it past Valdez to send someone.

The bodies had been hauled off with no trouble, however, and he was glad of it. He wasn't sure why, but even MacCorkendale seemed to have relinquished control of the situation and looked to Slocum to be told what to do.

With Curly on guard, Slocum set MacCorkendale and Bill to setting posts again, while he and Juan followed with the wire. They made good time, and while they all agreed that it didn't look like much, it was strong and would serve the purpose.

They made about four and a half miles that day, their best yet, and by the time they were done, Curly and his rifle had moved down a line of at least ten hills. He was also the only one who wasn't tired to the bone and sweated through.

They parted for the day. As usual, Slocum unhitched the

horses from the wagons and led them back to town. Tomorrow would be their last day of work, and also as usual, he would lead them back loaded with water and grain for the day.

He was glad to be nearly done with this mess. He wanted to wash his hands of it and relax and let his aching shoulder and punctured hands heal all the way. Possibly while he played cards and sipped champagne.

He and Juan had traveled perhaps a mile toward town, engaged in the lazy sort of small talk that tired men are prone to engage in, when he heard the echoing *pop* of a distant shot.

"That came from behind us," Juan said.

"Shit," Slocum muttered and quickly tossed Juan the string's lead ropes. "Get 'em back to town."

"Why?" asked a puzzled Juan.

"If you wanna live long enough to get hitched, just do it," Slocum shouted as he wheeled Concho and set off for the MacCorkendale place at a gallop.

Miguel Cordura had lazed away half the day waiting for Maria, then finally given up on the bitch. It was time that he got to work, and Valdez hadn't set out any particular order for the killings, had he?

And so Cordura had ridden out of town and toward the MacCorkendales' ranch. Once there, he had stayed just out of sight of the house for a good hour, watching to see who was home and what hands were around the place.

Once he was satisfied that there was only one woman in the house—MacCorkendale's wife, he supposed—and only one hand working lazily in the barn, he backtracked himself.

Far to the north and through binoculars, he watched Slocum and the others working on the fence. He couldn't see Jorgé—Valdez had been particularly insistent about getting Jorgé—but finally he decided that he would find

Jorgé later. He saw MacCorkendale and Slocum and Juan. Three out of four was not bad.

He did not want to attack when there were so many of them. There were also a couple of other Anglos, probably from MacCorkendale's ranch, and he had no idea how clever any of them were with a gun. He had been warned about Slocum, however, and Jorgé? Jorgé went without saying. He was not famous for nothing.

He waited.

And waited.

And waited.

And finally, at long last, they stopped for the day.

He decided to follow MacCorkendale first. He would be the easiest to pick off from a distance, anyway. He would take care of Slocum and Juan later. Perhaps he could follow them into town and shoot them in their sleep.

Miguel Cordura was not a pistolero. He was more comfortable shooting from a distance or under the cover of darkness. He did not mind the killing, but let other men revel in the glory. He had known of too many men who had come to a bad end—and much too early in their careers—because they had gained fame with a gun.

Fools.

And so he trailed after MacCorkendale at a distance and to the north. He waited until they had gone about three-quarters of a mile before he rode up on a little breast of land, dismounted, and steadied himself and his gun with its telescopic sight on a large, flat rock.

He took careful aim at MacCorkendale, the only man in a green shirt. He kept bobbing behind one of the other men, and Cordura cursed beneath his breath, wishing for a clean shot.

And then, at last, he had it.

He took careful aim, adjusted for wind and distance, and pulled the trigger.

A moment later, he had the gratification of seeing Mac-

Corkendale fall from the saddle, and his men abruptly go to his aid. MacCorkendale was not moving, so far as he could see.

I am good, all right, he thought to himself and smiled.

One down, three to go.

In the firm knowledge that he was too far from them to be seen without an artificial aid or touched by anything less than his long-distance rifle, he leisurely packed away his gun sight and stand, stepped up on his horse again, and started slowly back the other way toward town.

You know, he thought as he set out at a walk, so as not the raise any dust, *Valdez would have saved himself a great deal of both time and money if he had simply assigned this task to me in the first place.*

He shook his head. Why did employers always think that outside help was better, when they had the best working right there, all along?

Far to the south, Slocum galloped right past Cordura, neither seeing nor being seen. When he reached MacCorkendale, both Bill and Curly had their guns out and were pointing them in every conceivable direction, mostly his.

He reined Concho down to a halt, said, "Hold up there, boys," and stepped down to the ground. Before him lay MacCorkendale, who, at first, Slocum thought was dead. Blood covered his right arm and side, and Slocum went to him immediately.

He was about to ask the men where he was hit, but it was apparent. A slug had torn into his upper arm and passed through to enter his side. He was losing a lot of blood, and it looked to Slocum as if the slug had penetrated his lung.

To Bill, he said, "Ride to town. Get the doc. And hurry."

Then to Curly, he said, "Help me."

While Bill sped off to town, he and Curly managed to get a tourniquet around MacCorkendale arm, pack the wound in his side, and hoist him up and across his saddle. Slocum snugly tied him to the saddle with Curly's rope.

Slocum would have vastly preferred a travois, but there was no wood around, other than some scrawny brush here and there. They'd just have to travel slow and easy and try not to do MacCorkendale any more damage than had already been done.

"Did you see where it came from?" Slocum asked as they started out, MacCorkendale on his horse between them.

"Out there, somewhere," answered Curly, pointing to the north. "He was a good ways out. Couldn't see hide nor hair of the son of a bitch."

His tone, while bitter, was full of concern for MacCorkendale, who, in his semiconscious state, was coughing up blood.

It was not a good sign.

He looked over at Curly. "That horse Bill was ridin'. It fast?"

"Yeah," came Curly's answer. "He won the last founder's day race up in Bisbee, ol' Flash did."

"Good." Slocum stared at MacCorkendale. "Hope you're right."

20

Maria's worst fears were confirmed when she saw Bill Thibedoux thunder past the cantina, leap off his horse, and pound on the doctor's door. She knew he and Curly Ryan were to be out working with Slocum today.

She threw down the dish towel in her hands and raced out through the crowded cantina and into the street. "Bill!" she called as she ran toward the doctor's office. "Bill, what has happened?"

By the time she reached him, Dr. Oaty had already answered the door and been filled in, and was just leaving to fetch his buggy.

"Doc! Bill! Who is hurt? Is it Slocum?"

Bill wheeled toward her, and she nearly ran into him. "It's Mr. MacCorkendale, Maria. Somebody shot him, bad."

"And Slocum?"

"He's with Mr. MacCorkendale. Him and Curly are takin' him back to the ranch."

"Bill, you must take a message to Slocum for me," Maria began, and briefly described the man who had been in the cantina earlier, and who had finally left after he grew tired of her stalling.

"Aw, shit!" Bill said, then quickly added, "Sorry, Miss Maria. But from what you say, I'll bet anythin' that that was Cordura. Miguel Cordura. He works for Valdez. He was an awful bad man in his day, and men that bad don't change their stripes. Plus, Mr. MacCorkendale was shot from far off. That was Cordura's speciality."

"And Señor Valdez would probably be angry enough to send him?"

"Yes, ma'am, I reckon he would."

Just then Doc Oaty came flying around the corner in his buggy and hollered, "You comin' or not, Bill?"

Without a further word to Maria, Bill vaulted onto his gelding's back and kicked him into a gallop, leaving her alone and standing in a billow of slowly drifting dust.

Juan, trailing a string of horses, rode into town about a half hour later, and after depositing them at the livery, decided to go not to Conchita, and not to see Jorgé—who would probably be doing something with that crazy lady, Samantha—but to go to the cantina. Maria, he thought, should know why Slocum was delayed.

And besides, he was thirsty.

"Cerveza," he announced to Diego, who was working the bar.

Maria immediately came out from the kitchen, hurried down the length of the bar, and threw her arms around him.

Startled, he hopped back and said, "Maria!"

"Thank the Blessed Virgin you live, Juan!" she cried, and clasped her hands before her.

"I am fine, Maria," he said, still a little goggle-eyed. "It is someone from the MacCorkendale's ranch that is not so well. That is what I have come to tell you."

She nodded quickly. "I talked to Bill. He came for the doctor. It is Señor MacCorkendale himself who is wounded. It is bad, Bill said."

"Madre de Dios," Juan muttered, looking at the floor. "I

am very sorry to hear this news. Señor MacCorkendale can be bullheaded, but he is a fine fence stringer." He looked up and seemed to remember himself. "Slocum, Maria. That is what I have come to say. Slocum rode back when we heard the shot. I do not know where he is."

"Bill told me that he and Curly took Señor MacCorkendale back to his rancho."

"And no word of the pistolero who shot Señor MacCorkendale?"

Maria filled him in with what details she knew—which weren't many—and Juan nodded sagely. "I know of this Miguel Cordura. He is very bad, and a crack shot. At least, he still must be. I have not heard anything of him for many years now. Perhaps he has been hiding in the employ of Señor Valdez under a different name."

"Perhaps." Maria excused herself and wandered back to the kitchen. She had a full house tonight, and the place was packed with diners and drinkers. But as she opened the kitchen door, she could hot help but worry about Slocum.

Where had the pistolero, Miguel Cordura, gone? Was he, at this very moment, closing in on Slocum? What a coward he was, to shoot from so far!

Or perhaps he had come into town again, to prey upon Juan and Jorgé. A shiver ran through her, and when Diego came back to fetch dinner plates, she whispered, "Tell Juan to be extra careful tonight. Tell him that Cordura may be in town."

And as Diego left, burdened by plates, she added, "And tell him to warn Jorgé and his woman, as well!"

Jorgé, who couldn't do much more than watch out the window, had seen Juan come into town. Alone.

And he was getting more than a little nervous about it.

"A problem, my love?" asked Samantha, looking up from her magazine.

"Why?"

"You growled." She smiled at him.

"Ah. Perhaps I did. For now, it is nothing, my dove. Do not worry your pretty head about it."

She gave a little shrug and said, "All right, honey."

If the truth were told, aside from her physical charms—which were great, indeed—what attracted Jorgé to her the most was, well, her stupidity.

He valued that in a woman. He liked them silly and dense and self-absorbed and not at all in tune with the true ways of the world.

And Samantha was that.

He found her quite charming, although he knew that Slocum disagreed with him. Slocum liked smart women. Well, in that way, Jorgé thought that Slocum was a fool. Women should know nothing of men's business. They should be content to cook and clean and spread their dimpled knees, and be happy about it.

"Honey?" she asked.

"What, my dove?"

"You want I should go across the street and ask them to send over some supper?" She set aside her magazine. "Or do you feel like walkin' over there?"

"Yes," he said. "To the first. Have them send us some supper, and have them send champagne, too. We will dine in luxury tonight."

Samantha giggled and came to him, her hand out for money. She asked, "You want your regular?"

Miguel Cordura had been in town for several hours. He knew which room Jorgé was in, and that he was with a woman. He'd watched Juan's entrance into Jaguar Hole, as well, and his journey to the cantina.

Two prairie fowl, ripe for the plucking.

He had tethered his horse in a patch of shade behind him, out back of the mercantile, and currently sat in the shadowy mouth of an alley, just two doors down from Cantina Lopez. Juan had walked right past him.

But Cordura was thinking, not shooting, for the time being. If he could find a way to get the two of them together—Juan and Jorgé—it would make things much simpler. Simpler targets, simpler escape.

There would be no time between shootings for the town to get itself aroused and riled up, for overly brave shopkeepers to arm themselves and make more people for him to shoot.

Not that he minded, but he was only being paid for Slocum, MacCorkendale, Juan, and Jorgé. And ammunition was expensive.

It felt good to kill again, to do what he was born to do. He had been retired—against his will—for almost ten years, now, ten years he had spent in the employ of Señor Valdez. He did not know why Valdez had not just sent him out after MacCorkendale in the first place, unless Valdez, who knew of his past, was trying to protect him.

No, it would not be that, he decided. That was too thoughtful to expect from a man like Valdez.

It was probably because Valdez did not trust his skills, thought Cordura had grown lazy or rusty or lost his gift of marksmanship.

Despite himself, he smiled, there in the shadows. To think that a man such as he would ever lose his skills with a rifle or a gun! Just because a man might go for years without riding a horse, did that make him a beginner once he was mounted again?

Of course not!

Jorgé's gringa woman came out of the hotel, and Cordura watched as she crossed the street. The great Jorgé Rodriguez would be alone, now. Cordura could shoot him now, through his window.

But that still left the problem of Juan. He thought for a

moment, decided to take his chances with a town massacre, and stepped out into the street.

But not far. He leapt back, for Juan had exited the cantina and was going across to the hotel!

Cordura sat down again. It would be wonderful luck if he went to visit Jorgé, would it not?

He watched carefully as Juan entered the building, and then he switched his line of vision up to Jorgé's window. He would wait and see.

Jorgé looked up at the sound of a knock on the door. "Samantha?" he called. "Back so soon?"

But the voice from outside was definitely not Samantha's.

"Jorgé, we must talk!"

"Come in then, Juan."

When Juan shut the door behind him, Jorgé saw fear on his face. "What is it, amigo?"

"Someone shot Señor MacCorkendale. From far off. Slocum has gone to help take him to his rancho, and I think maybe the one who did it is Miguel Cordura. And I would get back from that window if I were you, Señor Rodriguez."

Jorgé immediately scooted away from the open window. "When did all this happen, Juan?"

"Just now. In the last hour, maybe, more or less."

"Where'd Cordura come from? I thought he died years ago!"

Juan shook his head. "No, no, Señor Rodriguez! He has worked for Señor Valdez for many years, now. You do not remember Miguelito, from the rancho?"

Jorgé *did* remember him. That lazy oaf, always finding somewhere else to be when there was hard work to be done, that had been Miguel Cordura? He had never met the man before, only heard his reputation. They said that in his day, he could shoot the eyes from a fly at two hundred yards.

He had owned a fabled rifle, especially built for him,

with a telescopic sight and a metal stand to hold it steady. Jorgé had seen Miguelito with a rifle, but never one that special. Perhaps it came apart, the stand and the telescope, to just leave the rifle? He did not know. He knew only that this meant trouble.

Valdez would not be stopped.

"Juan, why, when Señor Valdez had Miguel Cordura working for him all along, would he bother himself to find me?"

Juan shook his head. "Maybe he thinks Cordura is no good anymore?"

"Maybe," said Juan.

Cordura would have to be in his late fifties or early sixties. Most men lost their taste for killing before that age.

Either that, or they, themselves, were killed.

Jorgé leaned forward to get his crutch. And in that split second, the window exploded and the force of a slug pushed him sideways, sprawling, chair and all, onto the floor.

Almost before he had time to register that he had been hit, Juan came scurrying toward him, and he heard himself shout, "Get down!" even as another shot rang out. Juan stood for a second, frozen in shock, and then toppled to the floor.

Jorgé reached for him with his good arm, fingers creeping across the floor to the man's shoulder. "Juan!" he hissed. "Juanito!"

Juan did not move.

Jorgé heard the pounding of hoofbeats galloping away, fading into the distance, and knew there was nothing that could be done to catch the shooter. Not now, anyway. And then he heard Samantha down on the street, crying, "Jorgé!" and the sound of her little shoes running toward the hotel from across the way.

Moments later she pushed open the door, took one look inside the room, and began to scream.

21

Slocum and Helga sat stiffly in the parlor while Dr. Oaty worked upstairs on Ralph MacCorkendale.

MacCorkendale had come to about ten minutes out from the house and had hollered so much that he made himself pass out again. It was just as well, Slocum figured. Now was a real good time for him to be unconscious.

He didn't know exactly what the doc was doing to Ralph, but he was certain that it had to hurt like hell. Ralph had been busted up pretty bad, and the doc said he was going to have to set his arm and dig a slug out of his lung.

Everybody Slocum had known before who had suffered a shot to the lung had died.

He didn't mention this to Helga, though. She sat on the opposite side of the room like a statue, her head turned from him. Still, he could see the silent tears falling slowly down her cheeks.

She did care for Ralph, after all, he realized with some surprise. Then what the hell had been going on with that kiss the other morning?

Now wasn't the time to ask, though. And truth be told, he'd rather not know. So he just sat there.

Until he and Helga both jerked toward the sounds of

something metal hitting the floor above, and then Ralph's curses.

Slocum started to stand up while the battle upstairs escalated, but Helga motioned him down again and quickly hurried from the room and up the steps. Slocum quietly followed her but stopped in the foyer and watched her go along the open upstairs hall to the master bedroom.

The hollering stopped the moment she opened the door. Which probably left Doc Oaty fairly relieved, as just prior to that, MacCorkendale had been threatening to castrate him with a rusty pocket knife.

Or at least, that's what it sounded like to Slocum. It was a little hard to tell with all the intermingled curses and yelps of pain, and the barking "Shut up, Ralph!"s from the doc.

"Everything all right up there?" Slocum asked when Helga came out a moment later.

"Ja," she said as she made her way down the hall to the head of the stairs. "Ralph has much pain. But the doctor says that he thinks he will be all right. It will take much bed rest and nursing."

She turned the corner of the landing and started down the stairs. "The swearing, that came when the morphine wore off," she added. "Dr. Oaty has given him more. He sleeps now."

"That's good," Slocum replied as she walked down to his level, then started for the kitchen. "I make coffee now. You would maybe like something to eat?"

"Don't trouble yourself, ma'am." He was still standing in the foyer. "I'd best get myself back to town. Got a couple friends there that need to be warned about this feller that shot up Ralph."

She turned toward him, her hand on the kitchen door. "Why, Slocum? Why do these men do these things?"

He shook his head. "I don't know, Helga."

"I think they do not, either," she said softly and walked into the kitchen and out of his sight.

Concho had been fed and watered and was eager to be off again when Slocum saddled him. At least someone was happy, Slocum thought as he tightened the cinch.

He sure wasn't. MacCorkendale was probably going to live, but he had been just plain lucky. The doc had said a half inch farther to the side, and that slug could have exploded his heart.

And Slocum had no idea where Ralph's assailant was. He might be out there, hiding somewhere along the trail, or he could already be in town, hunting down Jorgé and Juan.

Then again, he might have just gone home, since his main target—at least, Slocum assumed MacCorkendale was the main target—had been taken down.

Of the three options, Slocum was betting his money on the last one. He had to. He needed to get to Jorgé and Juan.

The sun was most of the way down when he started out, but he traveled at a gallop. Concho was surefooted and smart. And careful. Slocum gave him his head, let him run, and trusted the Lord that he wouldn't step in a badger's den or a prairie-dog hole.

Then, when he was nearly halfway to town, Concho went down.

Slocum was catapulted free of the saddle and scrambled out of the thrashing horse's way, cursing himself and whatever had made the hole the horse had stepped in, when he heard the distant report of a shot.

And he knew he'd made the wrong bet. Whoever had shot Ralph MacCorkendale was out there right now and probably had Slocum in his sights.

He lay very still, silently cursing Valdez and whoever he'd hired to do this. The man had done worse than shot

Slocum. He'd killed Concho. The horse heaved his final, rattling breath while Slocum lay there, unable to help him, unable to do anything except mutter, "Sorry, old son. Sorry, boy."

He thought fast, shoving his grief aside for the moment. He could move and try to get back around the son of a bitch. But chances were that if the bastard could see well enough to kill his horse from wherever he was, he'd surely see Slocum coming. He must have a rifle with a telescopic sight; that was all Slocum could figure.

Very slowly, he inched his hand toward his gun belt and drew his pistol. It would be no good to him now, but maybe, just maybe, the shooter would come down to check on his handiwork.

And if he did, Slocum would have a little surprise for him. The goddamn horse killer.

Five minutes. Seven. Fifteen.

The son of a bitch was taking his time, all right.

Slocum considered standing up. Maybe he was gone.

But then, maybe he'd just been so far out that it was going to take him a while longer.

Better safe than sorry, he supposed. He lay still and waited.

More than twenty-five minutes after he'd fired the shot that killed Concho, the son of a bitch sniper came close enough for Slocum to hear his approaching hoofbeats. He was walking, plodding nearer and nearer.

At last, when he was close enough that Slocum could hear the creak of his saddle leather and the soft breaths of his mount, he stopped. Slocum waited for him to dismount but was disappointed.

What's he going to do? Shoot me from the saddle, just to make sure I'm dead? Slocum thought angrily.

He heard a gun cock and almost leapt to his feet when

he heard the complaint of saddle leather. The bastard was getting down, after all.

He held very still, the gun in his hand hidden beneath his aching shoulder.

He heard a soft chuckle. "Two for the price of one, eh?" a gruff male voice said. "Just so you will know, spotted horse, you are the reason Slocum is as dead as you. I would have seen that spotted coat from miles away."

The muscles of Slocum's jaw clenched involuntarily.

Dirt sprayed his nose as the killer stepped to stand over him. "Break your neck, fancy man?" he asked, rhetorically. "Your reputation, she turned out to be bigger than you were, no?"

"No, you goddamn horse murderer!" Slocum shouted as he suddenly rolled and fired. His slug went directly into the killer's heart, angling up to sever his spine.

He fell forward, on top of Slocum, who wriggled free, still cursing.

And when he gained his feet, he kicked savagely at the corpse over and over again, taking pleasure in the sound of the dead man's ribs breaking. He wanted to pound him into nothing.

Finally, when he was himself again, he turned to Concho. He knelt next to the animal, stoking his glossy neck a final time. The slug had taken him just in front of the girth, probably ricocheting around inside him to slice up all his major organs.

At least he'd died fast.

Slocum wished he could have made his killer's death last a whole lot longer.

He pulled his saddlebags free and tied them on the killer's horse, then did what he could to strip off Concho's tack. He couldn't pull the saddle all the way free, but he got the bridle off and tossed it aside.

And then, without a backward glance at the dead man's

corpse, Slocum mounted his bay horse and trotted off toward town.

Had the killer been there already? He'd had time. Slocum urged the horse into a gallop.

He reached town in slap time, stopped at the livery only long enough to give instructions for the kid there to walk the bay out for a half hour, and loped up the street toward the cantina.

He was ten feet inside the door when Maria rushed into his arms and embraced him tightly.

"What?" he said. "What is it?" He noted that the mood in Cantina Lopez seemed odd somehow. The crowd was thin, and everybody seemed jumpy. He held Maria out at arm's length. "Was he here, Maria?"

Without asking who he meant, she said, "*Sí, sí*, he was."

"And Jorgé? Juan?"

Tears in her eyes, she pointed out the door, across the street toward the hotel.

"Shit," he breathed, and took off running.

22

There were two women in the hotel room, and both of them were crying. Samantha Rollings was the first. The second one Slocum took to be Conchita, Maria's sister. Anyway, she was hovering over Juan and feverishly praying for him in Spanish.

At first, Slocum couldn't tell whether Juan was dead or alive. Jorgé was fine, though, relatively speaking. He knew it right off, when Jorgé lifted his head from the pillow and grumbled, "As always, amigo, you are too goddamn late."

He also knew that Jorgé was wounded pretty bad, from the amount of blood covering his shirt and his sheets.

"Juan?" Slocum asked.

Jorgé shook his head and said, "Wait."

Two other men had come into the room and were occupied with moving Juan to another room. Conchita followed them, wailing.

When they were gone, Slocum closed the door and asked, "What happened?"

Jorgé tried to shrug and ended up grimacing instead. "Somebody shot us through the window. We have no proof, but I think it was Miguel Cordura. He works for Señor—"

"Cordura?" Slocum broke in. He remembered Cordura's name from way back. "I thought he was dead!"

"It seems not. He works for Señor Valdez. I saw him there, but I did not make the connection."

Slocum ground his teeth, then said, "Worked for Valdez, you mean. He ain't workin' for nobody anymore."

Jorgé's eyes narrowed. "Tell me."

By the time Slocum walked back into the cantina, it was fully dark outside, his stomach was growling, and the doctor had arrived back in town and was working on Juan.

It seemed he wasn't as near death as Jorgé had thought, but it was still going to be touch and go. It had fallen to Slocum to escort Conchita away, so that Doc Oaty could do his work.

Jorgé was next in line, and together, Slocum and Samantha had managed to slow the flow of blood down to a mere trickle while he waited his turn.

Slocum had told Samantha that he was proud of her. He meant it, too.

He might be wrong, but he was pretty well convinced that Samantha had actually fallen for Jorgé.

The crowd at Cantina Lopez was even thinner and more sedate when he ushered Conchita inside. Conchita was a lot like her sister, although she probably had an extra thirty pounds on her, and she wasn't as tall. But she still had those gorgeous sloe eyes and that coffee-and-cream skin, and the long, silky, raven's wing hair.

She was a looker, too.

They found a table and waited for Diego to take their orders, which Maria eventually brought to the table herself. She also brought her own dinner, and pulled out a chair.

Maria immediately put an arm around her sister's shoulders and asked, "How is Juan, Conchita?"

Conchita sniffed and replied, "He lives. The doctor says it will be a long time until he is himself, though. Oh,

Maria, he was nearly killed!" She covered her face with her hands and began to cry again.

Maria flicked a glance toward Slocum before she said, "Yes, Conchita, but he still lives! Is it not wonderful? Should we not celebrate for Juan?"

Conchita wagged her head, behind her hands. "Every time a man falls in love with me, he is shot!"

"Hell, Conchita, I know a whole lot of men got themselves shot and never even *met* you!" Slocum said.

Despite herself, Conchita's giggle escaped through her fingers, and Maria smiled broadly at Slocum and reached over to take his hand. "This is true, Conchita," she said.

"And Juan is avenged, Conchita," Slocum added. "The man who shot him and Jorgé tried to take me out tonight, on my way into town. He's dead, now."

The memory of it was maddening, and he dropped Maria's hand before he crushed her fingers. He picked up his cerveza and took a long drink.

"This is true?" both Conchita and Maria said at the same time.

"True," said Slocum staring down at his plate. He picked up his fork and cut off a bite of enchilada, but he was too angry to eat, despite his rumbling stomach.

Maria said, "Slocum, what is wrong? Did you know this man? Was he a friend of yours?"

"Hardly." How could he admit that the rage he felt was because Cordura had killed his horse? Not because he had nearly killed three good men, friends of his, but because of the horse.

It was something he expected practically no one would understand. No one except possibly Maria—and Jorgé, who he'd already told—but certainly not her sister.

Gently, Maria said, "It is done, my Slocum. Whatever there was, it is now over and done."

He looked up and shook his head. "No," he said. "There's still Valdez."

• • •

Salma Valdez carried a small tray up the stairs to her husband. On it was one of his favorite cigars, a decanter of port and a crystal goblet, and a small plate of the special sugar cookies he liked so much.

She tapped at the door and announced herself, then walked in without waiting for a reply. Valdez was propped up in bed and putting a marker in the book he had been reading.

"I thought you might like a little something, my love," she said with a smile.

"How kind, Salma," he replied, and patted the edge of the bed. "Come and sit beside me."

She did, and put the tray on his bedside table. He reached for the cigar first, as she had known he would, and made a show of trimming and lighting it. She smiled sweetly through all of it. Pablo was a boy, really, and now he was showing off for her with his little ceremony with the cigar. She found it endearing.

She also had something to tell him, something that would make him very happy. She had tried to tell him the other afternoon, when they had walked through the gardens with their fragrant roses, but he had seemed distant. He was probably still thinking about the fence.

How foolish, how asinine, to spend so much time and energy fussing over a simple fence! It seemed perfectly natural to her. But this was a new land, and sensibilities were different here. She knew that.

She also knew that sensibilities had to change—both those of countries and people. She was proud of Pablo for trying, for making the effort to change.

He puffed at his cigar gratefully, then set it down to pour himself a glass of port and snatch a cookie from the plate. "How nice," he said. "You had them make my favorites."

"Always, Pablo. How are you feeling?"

"I will be better once I have had a glass of this port," he replied, taking a sip, then another. "I think your 'magic' medicines are working though, Salma. This is not the first time I have been wounded, but this is the best I have felt afterwards. *Muchas gracias, querida.*"

She leaned forward, and he kissed her lips.

"I am very proud of you, Pablo."

He appeared surprised. "Me? What have I done?"

It was her turn to be surprised. "Why, the fence, my darling. You have decided not to interfere any further."

He looked away, and she frowned. Just what had he been up to that she had not been told about?

"Pablo?"

He tipped his glass back and drained it.

"Pablo?" she repeated.

"I would like to be alone now, my peach," he muttered.

"Pablo, what have you done?"

He turned toward her and suddenly barked, "I said I would like to be alone. Now!"

She stood up and stalked from the room without one further word, and slammed the door behind her. He *had* done something, something that would undoubtedly lead to more bloodshed. And all over a few stupid cows!

She had great news to tell him, something wonderful, but now she never wished to tell him at all. She wished, in fact, that she could go home to her mother.

But her mother had been dead for many years, now, and there was no home to go to. No home, except here.

Perhaps her sister would take her in? No, she and Raquel had never gotten along. But there were cousins, back in France . . .

In any case, she would not tell Pablo now.

He did not deserve to know.

After Salma left, Pablo Valdez was at first consumed with anger at her, then anger at himself for being angry at her, and finally with wondering why Miguel Cordura had not checked in with him yet.

It was long past dark. Surely Cordura would not spend the night out on the range after his labors, when he had the bunkhouse to rest in.

But he would most certainly not go the bunkhouse without seeing his *patrón* first!

So he must not have come in, then.

Perhaps he had been right about Cordura all along. He was too old, too out of practice. He should have sent for someone else. He should have sent for someone besides Jorgé Rodriguez in the first place, that was what he should have done!

He sighed heavily and felt pain shoot through his shoulder. Damn. Everything was so much simpler in hindsight, was it not?

And now he had angered Salma.

About this, he felt very bad. But he had been frustrated and angry, and could not take the words back.

He poured himself a fresh glass of port, and proceeded to smoke and drink.

And fume and simmer.

Miles away in Jaguar Hole, Slocum stood in Jorgé's hotel room. Jorgé had been patched up and now bore a cast on his arm as well as his leg. He was not one bit happy about it.

And he was drinking laudanum like there was no tomorrow.

"Better slow down on that stuff," Slocum warned.

"Oh, go to hell," Jorgé replied, and took another swig from the medicine bottle.

"He's a grown man, Slocum," Samantha said softy. "He knows how much he needs."

"Damn right, honey," Jorgé announced. "You're a good woman, Samantha. You always take your man's side of things."

Samantha smiled sweetly.

Slocum wanted to be sick.

But he bit his tongue and said, "Jorgé, I'm ridin' out to Valdez's place in the mornin'."

Jorgé cocked a brow. "You are going to kill him?"

Slocum shook his head. "I'm goin' to try and talk some sense into the son of a bitch. But I'll kill him if he pushes me. He's responsible for MacCorkendale and you and Juan. Not to mention his own men dyin'. And Concho."

"You are a fool, Slocum, but this goes without saying." Jorgé shrugged. "How goes it with Juan? Have you checked on him?"

"No, but Conchita's in there now. She ain't screamed, so I guess he's still breathin'."

"Well, that is something, amigo."

"Yeah. Hope he makes it through the night."

"If Conchita stays at his side, he will not die." Again, Jorgé sipped at the laudanum. "He will live, for her."

Before Jorgé had a chance to get sloppy about love or laudanum, Slocum got down to business.

He sat down in a wooden chair next to the bed, pulled out a scrap of paper and a piece of lead he'd borrowed from Diego, and said, "All right, how many men does he have out there, and what should I be prepared for?"

"Slocum?"

"Yeah?"

"Again, I am sorry about your horse."

23

The next morning, after one of Maria's trademark breakfasts, and after checking over at the hotel, Slocum set out for the MacCorkendale place.

Helga came to the door and ushered him upstairs. MacCorkendale was doing some better, although he still wasn't out of the woods, not by a long shot.

"Juan died sometime during the night," Slocum said after he sat down.

"Died?! I didn't even know he was sickly!" MacCorkendale said. His voice was hoarse with pain and painkillers.

Slocum explained the events that had transpired since he'd left the ranch last night, and MacCorkendale was visibly moved by it.

"So I came to see how you were and to borrow a horse," Slocum finished up.

"Why borrow a—" MacCorkendale began, and then said, "Oh, yeah."

"I rode Cordura's horse out this far. Gonna pack his body on it and haul it back to Valdez, but I need somethin' to ride myself. And not no stable horse. Don't suppose you got a good-broke Appy on the place?"

MacCorkendale half smiled. “Sorry, my friend. Got a nice chestnut gelding out in the barn, though. Will he do for a while?”

“Yeah.” Slocum stood up. “I’m pleased to find you doin’ so well, Ralph.”

“Same to you, Slocum. Seems to me this job turned out to be more than I thought it was going to. You, too, I’ll bet.”

“Yeah,” said Slocum, opening the door. He let himself out into the hall and turned back to tip his hat. “Be seein’ you, Ralph.”

He hoped that last part was the truest sentence he’d ever spoken.

He went out to the barn, and Bill directed him to the chestnut, one of three stabled there. The red gelding’s name was Scoot, and he had three white socks, with a snip and a star on his handsome face. The only thing that would have made him nicer was a snowflake blanket, Slocum thought as he saddled him up.

He had purposely veered wide of the place where he’d killed Cordura the night before. It didn’t have anything to do with Cordura himself, but with the horse he lay alongside.

And now, as he approached the scene, he felt fresh anger welling in his veins. He wasn’t any too gentle as he heaved Cordura’s stiff and smelling body over his horse’s saddle, and none to careful with the tie-down ropes, either. Cordura didn’t deserve any respect, alive or dead.

Once he had the body tied down to his satisfaction, he headed south, toward Mexico.

After he dealt with Valdez, he’d go back and cover Concho’s corpse with plenty of brush, then set it aflame. It was the best end for a good horse. A good bit more honorable than being coyote food, anyhow.

He followed the path he had taken before, and this time

there were no snipers in the canyon. It took him about three hours to reach the Valdez rancho.

He paused outside the big arch that announced Rancho Valdez, the letters ornate and burnt into the wood. He scanned the hacienda, so much grander than anything Ralph MacCorkendale ever dreamt of having, looked out over the close-in fields and corrals, the outbuildings.

Everything looked quiet.

He hoped it would stay that way.

He gave the chestnut a little nudge and passed under the arch at a jog, leading Cordura's bay along beside him. No one bothered him or even noticed that he was there.

He rode straight up to the big house, tied the horses to the porch rail, and walked up to the front door. He realized he hadn't been completely unnoticed when he lifted his knuckles to rap at the door, and a women opened it before he had a chance.

"May I help you?" she asked. She was a world-class beauty, too fair to be Mexican, and her accent was odd, part Spanish in places, part French. Was this Valdez's wife? If so, he had wed far above his station.

"My name's Slocum, ma'am," he began, sweeping his hat off. "And I work for—"

"Señor MacCorkendale, yes, I know," she said, and stepped aside, opening the door wider. "Come in, come in, please. I have heard all about your fence."

She didn't seem too pissed off about it, he thought, so he stepped inside. She led him to a room, a grand parlor of sorts, and rang a little bell that summoned a servant.

"Would you care for wine, Señor Slocum? Port, perhaps? And a cigar?"

Surprised by her hospitality, he managed to say, "A cigar'd be right welcome, ma'am, and just a glass of water, if you don't mind."

She sent the servant away and turned to him again, smiling.

"How's . . . how's Senñor Valdez doin'?" he asked. He figured that anything he said would get him into real trouble, so he asked about her husband first.

But she continued to smile. "His wound has slowed him somewhat. If you ask me, he deserved an artificial brake of some sort."

Puzzled, Slocum said, "What? I mean, beg pardon, ma'am?"

"Señor Slocum, I know all about your proposed fence, and I think it is a good idea. My husband, however, can be very . . . stubborn."

Well, that was a nice way to put it, Slocum thought.

"Señora Valdez," he said slowly, "I didn't come alone."

She cocked her head.

"Outside, tied to the rail, I brought back one of your hands. He's dead. Señora Valdez sent him to kill me and my friends. One's dead already, and two aren't lookin' very good. In fact, Ralph MacCorkendale is just holdin' on by the skin of his teeth."

Salma Valdez covered her mouth in shock. "I had no idea," she finally said, albeit in a whisper. "How could he have done this? How could he even have thought of it? I am so very sorry, Señor Slocum. I apologize for him. I am ashamed."

Slocum hesitated, then said, "Well, I sure thank you, ma'am. But I think I really need to speak with your husband."

"Of course, you do," she said, rising, and motioned him down when he started to stand as well.

The servant reappeared with a tall glass of water with a lemon wedge floating in it, and a good cigar. He placed both on the table beside Slocum.

"Stay here and enjoy your cigar, Señor Slocum, while I see if my husband is up to seeing visitors. If you please?" she added with a small curtsy, and left the room.

Classy lady, thought Slocum as he picked up the cigar. *Nothing but solid class.*

"And he has brought back the body of your man, Cordura," she said.

Valdez was so angry that it felt as if his insides were on fire. But before he could unclench his teeth to say a word, Salma added, "Pablo, if you do not see the sense in this thing, if you do not agree to do what Señor Slocum wishes, if you do not forever abide by this agreement, then I—and your unborn child—will be leaving. I still have cousins in France. They would be most pleased to take me in."

Suddenly, Valdez couldn't think of a complete sentence. He could only look at her and stutter, "Ch-child?" His dream of so many years, was it coming to pass after all? He could not believe his luck, this blessing!

And there Salma stood before him, her arms crossed resolutely over her chest and her toe tapping, angry with him when she should have been rejoicing with him, threatening him with stealing away his child when she should have been laughing and smiling and planning their new life as a family.

"Yes, Pablo, a child. Although it comes at a time when I begin to believe I do not know the man I married. Slocum says poor Juan is dead, and Señor MacCorkendale is holding on by only a thread. Shame on you! Shame!"

She looked furious, more angry than he'd ever seen her. But still, the only thing that escaped his lips was, "A child?"

She stared at him, her lips pursed.

"Yes, my dearest, my darling. Anything you say. I am most sorry. We will have the fence, I promise. We will live in peace with our good neighbors. When does it come, our joyous bundle?"

Finally, she smiled at him. It was like a sudden shower

when one has been in the desert for far too long. She said, "In the fall, Pablo. In October."

"You're gonna *what*?" Slocum asked. He feared his mouth was gaping and touched his chin to make sure.

Pablo Valdez, his beautiful wife at his elbow, sat up against a sea of pillows, and said, "You heard me, Slocum. I will send my own men to help with the fencing. My beautiful Salma," he said, taking her hand, "has made me see the error of my ways. I am heartily sorry for any pain I have caused."

Slocum didn't quite know what to say. Here, he'd been expecting to have a gun shoved in his face, and now this instead? He figured that maybe he ought to deal with the wives first, more often.

But he said, "Thank you, Señor Valdez. I'll pass on your good wishes. And I'm pretty sure MacCorkendale will send some of his men to help with the fence, too."

"Muchas gracias, Señor Slocum," said Salma Valdez. *"Merci beaucoup."*

"No, thank you to *you*," he replied with a nod of his head. "And you, Señor Valdez."

Valdez said, "My Salma tells me you ride a chestnut today. What has happened to your Appaloosa?"

The words cut through Slocum like a knife, but he managed to say, fairly calmly, "Your man killed him last night."

"Lo siento mucho," Valdez said, and actually appeared to be sorry. "It is hard to lose a good mount. I have an Appaloosa, down in the corral, just come in from Mexico City, so I do not know too much about him. He is a buckskin leopard, about four years old, though. It would please me greatly if you would take him, with my compliments."

Slocum nodded his head. "As you wish, Señor Valdez."

Ten minutes later found Slocum tacking up Valdez's buckskin leopard. He'd gone over the horse and found him sound and well made, suitable to his needs. When he asked one of the men what the horse's name was, the hand has said, "He does not have one. Just 'horse' I suppose."

"Well, that ain't much," Slocum mumbled to the horse. "I'll think you up one." He gave the cinch a final snug. "Don't count on nothin' too soon, though."

He left leading a horse again, but this time it was the chestnut he'd borrowed from Ralph, and there was no body tied across its back. Thank God. It might easily have been his.

In fact, he didn't rest easy until he'd crossed the border and ridden clear into the MacCorkendale spread. There, he conveyed the outcome of his talk with Valdez, and MacCorkendale agreed to send out three men to work on the fence the next morning. So far, so good.

MacCorkendale also paid him his fee. Five hundred dollars.

Sticking the bills in his pocket, Slocum said, "I'm gonna stick around town a couple more days, though, just in case. But I think your troubles are over."

"They are," MacCorkendale said and motioned him closer. "Don't tell Helga I told you, but I'm gonna be a daddy!"

"Well, congratulations, Ralph! That's great news." Indeed, MacCorkendale looked like he was about to bust his buttons. Slocum was genuinely happy for him. And Helga, too.

He left the ranch and slowly approached the place where Concho lay waiting. He dismounted about twenty feet out and slowly walked toward the horse, gathering dry brush and scrub as he went. He made quite a few trips out, gathering more brush, before he pulled the saddle clear. There was enough to make quite a blaze, which was what he needed.

He pulled out his sulphur tips and stood silently over the

horse for a moment before he said, "Thanks, Concho. You were a good one."

And then he lit a match and set the funeral pyre blazing.

It was dark by the time he reached Jaguar Hole. After stabling his new mount, he went up to the hotel to report to Jorgé.

"You are fooling me, Slocum!" he practically shouted. "He said he was sorry? He said he would send help?"

Slocum nodded. "Gave me a new Appy, too."

One-armed, Jorgé flung his hand skyward. "He has lost his mind! Or gained it. What do you suppose brought this on?"

"Don't know. But I got a feeling that Mrs. Valdez had somethin' to do with it."

"Ah, Señora Valdez . . . *Muy bonita.* No?"

Slocum grinned. "Very pretty, yes. Right nice, too."

"Yes, she is quite the lady." At Jorgé's side, Samantha frowned, and he quickly said, "As are you, my dove, as are you."

She smiled again and touched his brow fondly.

Slocum took that as a cue for him to leave. Maria was waiting, anyway. "I'll come see you tomorrow, Jorgé. Gonna hang around town for a bit. Might take a ride out to the fence tomorrow, too, just to see how the boys are gettin' on."

Jorgé nodded. "A wise idea. I wish I could go with you."

"Wish you could, too." Slocum stood up and headed toward the door.

"Thank you, Slocum," said Samantha softly, and he turned toward her. She looked as if she really meant it, and not just for stopping the border war. She clung to Jorgé like a tick to a hound.

He tipped his hat. "You're welcome, Miss Samantha. See you tomorrow, Jorgé."

As he crossed the street, thinking about a dozen things

at once, he came up with a name for the horse. One that would always remind him where he'd come from and what Slocum had gone through to get him.

Valdez.

He walked through the doors of the cantina filled with a sense of irony and how strange the world could be, and Maria jumped into his arms and kissed him soundly.

"You are alive, my darling," she cried happily and kissed him again.

He grinned. "Usually am, honey!"

Samantha watched out the window as Slocum crossed to the cantina. Yes, he was still handsome, yes, he still had those wide shoulders and those narrow hips, and yes, he still had that melting baritone voice.

But she had realized that the love of her life lay on the bed, beckoning to her. What good was it to be in love with a man who did not return the favor?

And Jorgé did. He had asked her to marry him that very afternoon and had shaken his head at her little silver ring. In fact, he had sent her out with fifty whole dollars to buy a gold one!

She loved Jorgé.

She would be with him forever.

Smiling, she turned away from the window and went to his side.

"Everything, it will be all right now?" Maria asked as she casually slung a long, cinnamon leg over Slocum's hip. It was late, and they had just finished making love. For the first time, anyway.

"Yes, Maria, I told you it will. 'Cept I'm worried about your sister."

"I am as well. She is taking Juan's death very hard."

Slocum nodded. "She should. Juan was a good man. He deserves to have somebody mourn him." He cupped her breast in his hand and kissed it, then looked up into her eyes. "When's the funeral?"

"Tomorrow, at two. Padre Francesco, he could not come today."

Slocum nodded. "Good. I'll be there. I'll pay for it, too, Maria. I promised to pay for his wedding. Seems the least I can do now . . ."

She smiled softly. He was quite a man, her Slocum. She said, "You are good."

He said, "And so are you, honey." Grinning, he pushed her onto her back.

"So soon?"

"Yeah, little darlin', so soon."

He entered her.

Don't miss a year of

Slocum Giant

by

Jake Logan

Slocum Giant 2004:

Slocum in the Secret Service

0-515-13811-8

Slocum Giant 2005:

Slocum and the Larcenous Lady

0-515-14009-0

LONGARM